CHRISTMAS AT COORAH CREEK

English nurse Katie Brooks is spending Christmas at Coorah Creek. She was certain that leaving London was the right decision, but her new job in the outback is more challenging than she ever imagined. Scott Collins rescued her on her first day and has been a source of comfort ever since. But he no longer calls the town home — it's too full of bad memories, and he doesn't plan on sticking around long. Scott needs to leave. Katie needs to stay. They have until Christmas to decide their future . . .

D0271154

Books by Janet Gover
in the Linford Romance Library:

BRING ME SUNSHINE

JANET GOVER

CHRISTMAS AT COORAH CREEK

Complete and Unabridged

LINFORD
Leicester

First published in Great Britain in 2015 by
Choc Lit Limited
Surrey

First Linford Edition
published 2018
by arrangement with
Choc Lit Limited
Surrey

A catalogue record for this book is available
from the British Library.

ISBN 978–1–4448–3937–1

Published by
F. A. Thorpe (Publishing)
Anstey, Leicestershire

Set by Words & Graphics Ltd.
Anstey, Leicestershire
Printed and bound in Great Britain by
T. J. International Ltd., Padstow, Cornwall

This book is printed on acid-free paper
For John, always

For John, always

Acknowledgements

I doubt very much that I could do this without the tremendous support I receive from my family and friends. You all know who you are and how much I love you.

For this book, special thanks go to my dear friend and a fabulous writer, Jean Fullerton, for her help with the nursing bits and to the wonderful Rachel Summerson for being a tough, but brilliant, critic and helping me become the best writer I can be.

Joining the Romantic Novelists' Association was the second best thing I've ever done — without the association and the friends I have made there, this would be a lonely journey indeed.

The very best thing I ever did was to fall in love with an Englishman with green eyes. Thanks for everything John.

Thank you also to the members of the Choc Lit Tasting Panel who enjoyed *Christmas at Coorah Creek*: Jennifer S., Cindy T, Lizzy, Linda Sp., Leanne F., Alma H., Helen D., Parama S., Sarah N. and Sharon M.

And last, but by no means least, thanks to the team at Choc Lit for loving my stories and taking such care with them, and to the Chocliteers — for being the best colleagues a girl could ever have.

1

In the middle of nowhere, Katie Brooks' car exploded.

At least that's how it felt as thick steam burst out from under the bonnet. Suddenly Katie was driving blind at high speed as the steam enveloped the front of her car. She lifted her foot from the accelerator and reached for the windscreen wipers. That only made things worse. The dust on her windscreen turned to mud and was smeared in a messy rust-coloured arc across the glass. Cursing, Katie turned the steering wheel and let the vehicle roll slowly to a stop on the side of the road. She got out and took a step back to look at the car she had owned for a little less than forty-eight hours. She didn't know much about cars, but she didn't need to know much to be certain that the blue Holden Commodore wasn't going anywhere in the near future.

'That'll teach me to buy a twenty year old car,' Katie muttered under her breath. 'So much for an 'Australian classic'. That's the last time I listen to a used car salesman.'

She took a deep breath and slowly turned in a circle.

She was standing in the middle of the longest stretch of straight flat road she had ever encountered. The thin grey line extended to the horizon in either direction, without so much as a building or another car in sight. In fact, she hadn't seen another human being for what seemed like hours. The only living thing she'd spotted was a kangaroo hopping across the road about a hundred miles back. So much space and so few people! Would she ever get used to it?

The geyser pouring from underneath her bonnet was beginning to ease. She opened the door and walked to the front of the car, reaching inside to feel for the catch. Very carefully she raised the bonnet, releasing another cloud of steam that quickly dissipated. She stared at her engine for a few seconds, before admitting it was a waste of time. She had no idea what to do. If she was going to get out of here, it wasn't going to be in the Commodore. She swung her leg to kick the offending vehicle, but at the last minute, pulled the blow. In her open-toed flat sandals, the kick was likely to hurt her foot more than the car.

She walked into the middle of the road and looked back the way she had come. Nothing. She looked in the direction she'd been heading. Somewhere out there was a small town called Coorah Creek. She did remember seeing a sign a while ago, but had no idea how far she still needed to go. And all the road signs were in kilometres, not miles. So even if she knew how many kilometres, she wasn't entirely sure she'd know how far that really was.

As she stood gazing down the road, bits from her reading leaped into the forefront of her mind. The bits about people dying of thirst when their cars broke down. And the bits about poisonous snakes and spiders. There probably weren't any man-eating crocodiles here, a million miles . . . kilometres . . . from the coast. But weren't the wild pigs dangerous too? Suddenly a whole less sure of herself, Katie leaned back against the car.

'Ow!' She leaped forward as the hot metal burned her thighs through the thin cotton of her skirt.

That was another thing. It was hot here. Really, really hot! Her car's on-again-off-again air-conditioning had barely been worth the name. And now she was standing in the blazing sun in an area desperately low on trees. She wandered along the road a short distance, looking for a tree big enough to give her a spot of shade. Nothing. She turned her face to the sky — a brilliant arc of totally cloudless blue. She could already feel her pale English skin starting to burn.

'Well,' she said to the vast empty spaces, 'I left cold, grey, miserable

London feeling burnt out by my job and that I'd lost my way. Now here I am, lost in the middle of nowhere and about to get really burned.'

The frustration building inside her suddenly exploded into a burst of laughter, but she was aware of the undertone of hysteria.

Returning to the car, she opened the rear door and rummaged around in the bags strewn over the back seat. Somewhere in there was a hat. And some sunscreen. Sweat was dripping from her forehead by the time she found them. She stepped back from the car and began slathering the white cream over her nose and cheeks.

'So now what do I do?' she wondered out loud. 'Do I wait with the car like it said in the books? Or do I start walking?'

The only answer was the distant haunting caw of a crow.

Surely someone would come along soon.

She reached for her handbag, and

retrieved her mobile phone. Squinting against the bright sunlight, she looked at it with little hope. She'd already discovered that large parts of Australia did not have mobile coverage. Either that or her phone was rubbish, which was also entirely possible.

Grimacing in disgust, she tossed the phone back onto the front seat.

Just a couple of weeks ago, she'd been wrapped in a heavy wool coat, fighting her way through crowds of shoppers in Oxford Street and admiring the best Christmas lights in London. She had cursed those crowds and their armloads of parcels and bags blocking her way. Right now she would give anything to see a few of them walking towards her. She would even offer to carry those parcels for them.

Once more she looked in both directions along the road. Nothing but the distant heat haze shimmering across the grey tarmac. It looked like water, or . . .

Water.

She was suddenly dying of thirst.

Katie turned back to her car. She wasn't a total idiot. She'd bought water at the last petrol station.

Ah-ha!

She held the plastic bottle aloft in triumph. But her joy was short lived. There was only about an inch of liquid left in the bottom. She removed the lid but hesitated. Should she drink it now or wait. Surely she wouldn't be here long? Would she?

Defiantly she drank the last of the water. There! It was done. Now someone had to find her.

She looked down at her arms, trying to see if the skin was already turning pink. It felt as if it should be. For the first time, she felt a real twinge of fear. As a nurse, she knew about the effects of sunstroke and dehydration. But what could she do? There wasn't any shade.

Maybe she could make her own.

She opened her suitcase and eventually found a long, light cotton skirt. She squinted up to judge the angle of the sun then opened both car doors. She tried to spread the skirt over them to form a tent. It didn't work. The patch of shade created wouldn't have sheltered a mouse. Even that little bit of effort had raised a sweat, and she could feel her energy being drained away by the relentless heat.

She looked at the skirt in her hands. It had been a gift from her sister, and she was quite fond of it. But she was also quite fond of being alive. If another car didn't come along for a couple of hours — and that seemed entirely possible — she was in real trouble.

She gripped the skirt firmly and tugged at the side seam. It took a lot of effort, but finally she heard the stitches tear. When she opened the skirt out, she had quite a large piece of fabric to work with. Enough to make some sort of tent. She spread the material between two open car doors, using the windows to hold the edges. After a few minutes work, and a lot more sweat, she had created a small patch of shade between the two doors, under the tented fabric.

Before she sat down, she scrabbled around some more in her suitcase, and emerged with a woolly cardigan — a garment she was unlikely to need in the near future. She put the cardigan down in the small patch of shade. That would give her bum some respite from the rough gravel on the side of the road. Then she lowered herself into her makeshift sun-shelter.

It wasn't cool. Far from it. The heat radiating from the metal of the car was intense, but at least she wasn't in the full blazing sun.

She wriggled about a bit. Trying to get comfortable — or at least less uncomfortable. She tried to stay focused, listening for the sound of an approaching engine. But all she could hear was that damn crow. It was starting to get on her nerves.

She glanced at her watch. How long had she already been here?

Her head was starting to spin and her eyelids fluttered.

No! She had to stay awake.

She shook her head, wishing she still had some water left. Wishing she had never hopped on that plane in London. She had really messed up. Again. The wrong career, and now the wrong place to pursue that career.

Her life wasn't exactly going as she had hoped. If only . . . .

She felt her eyelids starting to close. She took a deep breath and blinked rapidly. It already felt like she'd been stranded for hours. She glanced down at her watch again. Time was moving at a snail's pace.

She must not fall asleep!

2

It had to be the most boring stretch of road in the world — this road that led to Coorah Creek. This road that was taking him back after so many years. It was long and straight and flat with no turnings or side roads. Scott Collins wondered if maybe there was a metaphor in that.

He wriggled his fingers on the wheel to relieve the stiffness and the boredom. He'd never thought he'd see this part of the country again. And certainly not of his own volition. But times change. People change. He was coming back to Coorah Creek and he had no idea what was waiting for him there.

He reached out to pick up the water bottle from the centre console. His air-conditioning was going full bore, but he could still feel the sun beating down on his car. He was looking forward to getting away from the relentless heat. And the dull burnt colours. And the rain that thundered so hard on a tin roof that you couldn't hear yourself think. His future was full of lush green places, where rain fell in gentle refreshing showers. He might even get his first white Christmas, if things went well. That could be fun. He'd never seen snow.

At least he would be in a place where there were no memories to haunt him.

But if he was going to escape those memories, there was something he had to do first. He had to return to Coorah Creek.

Somewhere ahead of him, the sun flashed off metal, pulling Scott's attention back to the long straight road. It was easy — and very dangerous — to lose concentration like that. He strained to see through the shimmering heat haze in the distance. There was a dark shape — a car — on the side of the road up ahead.

Scott immediately lifted his foot from

the accelerator. He'd been away from the outback for more than eight years, but some lessons are never forgotten. In the outback, you never drove past a stranded car without stopping to see if the driver needed help. Out here, a broken down car could cost someone their life.

Scott pulled off the road a few yards behind the blue Commodore. He registered its make with a smile. The car was a classic, but getting on in years. He wasn't surprised that it was stuck way out here. Now, where was the driver?

That's when he noticed the fabric stretched between the two open doors. Someone had tried to construct a shelter. He strode quickly forward when he saw a girl apparently unconscious lying half in and half out of that makeshift shelter. He swiftly knelt beside her and reached out a hand to touch her face where the skin was already red. She looked so young and so terribly vulnerable.

13

'What the . . . ' With a jerk the girl suddenly sat up, her eyes staring wildly around her.

'Hey. It's all right.' Scott sat back on his heels to give the girl some breathing room.

She ran her hand over her face. Slowly her eyes came to focus on him. 'Oh.'

'I saw your car. Are you all right?'

'Yes. I fell asleep. Jet lag.' The words came out as a harsh croak.

'Hang on a second. Don't try to get up yet. You need water.'

Scott rose to his feet and jogged back to his car. The water bottle he'd been drinking from was half empty, but there were two more on the passenger seat. He picked up both of them.

The girl had pulled herself into a sitting position, leaning back against the car. She looked terrible. Scott tried to conceal his concern as he passed her an open bottle.

'Slowly,' he warned as she began gulping down the warm liquid. 'Slowly!' Scott put his hand on her arm and she lowered the bottle. 'If you drink too fast you'll probably throw up,' he told her. 'And we don't have enough water to waste it like that.'

The girl took a deep breath, and nodded. She leaned back and closed her eyes. Scott could see the strain on her face. He waited silently until she was ready to take a few more slow sips of water.

'Do you want to try to get up?'

She nodded.

'Okay. But take it easy.'

The girl really didn't need the warning. She was moving very slowly, and looked quite shaky as she gathered her feet under her. Scott stood up and reached down to help her. She was a small thing — light as a feather and barely up to his chin. She swayed a little, and he kept one hand on her arm until he was certain she wasn't going to fall down again.

She took another smaller drink of water, and finally looked him squarely in the face.

'Thank you.' Her voice sounded much stronger.

'Are you all right?'

'I think so,' she said. 'I must have fallen asleep. It was so hot.'

'You passed out,' Scott said. 'Dehydration and heat exhaustion will do that.'

'I know that,' the girl said. 'I'm a nurse.'

'A nurse? Then you should know better than to come out here without water.'

'In my part of the world, there isn't much chance of dying of lack of water by the side of a road.'

As she spoke, her accent finally registered. 'You're English?'

'I am.'

'Then what the hell are you doing out here all by yourself? And without water? This isn't England.'

'I know that,' the girl said, a touch of anger bringing a spark into her blue eyes. 'I had water. I ran out. I wasn't expecting this rubbish car to break down, was I?'

'It's not a rubbish car.' Scott tried to

16

hide his smile as the girl painfully shook the fist she'd just thumped the car with. 'It's just old. What happened?'

'It exploded.'

Scott raised an eyebrow. Obviously a girl given to understatement. As she sipped slowly from the bottle of water, he moved to the front of the car and checked under the bonnet.

It didn't take him long to figure it out.

'You've probably put a stone through your radiator.'

'I'd figured that out too.'

Scott was pleased to see the girl had produced a hat from somewhere and was now wearing it. The brim wasn't broad enough to give her face much protection, but it was better than nothing.

'So what do I do now?' she asked.

'You're heading to Coorah Creek?'

'How did you know?'

'That's where this road goes,' he told her. 'After the Creek, there's just Birdsville.'

'And after that?'

'The desert. You really don't want to go there — and especially not with this.' He patted the old Holden affectionately.

She smiled at that, and Scott caught a glimpse of the girl behind the stranded tourist. Now that her eyes were no longer wide with distress, they were a lovely shade of blue-grey. Her face was a bit red from the sun, but she was a very pretty girl. About his own age, he thought. And as for that accent — that was just a cuteness bonanza. He couldn't help but wonder what on earth a girl like this was doing heading for the Creek.

'So?'

Acutely aware that he had been caught staring, Scott tried to look efficient. 'I guess I'd better get you into town.'

'Can't I call the . . . whatever you call the Automobile Association out here?'

Scott smiled. 'No, actually.'

'Oh. No phone service.'

He nodded.

'Well, there must be a garage at Coorah Creek. Have they got a tow truck? You could send them back for me.'

The words froze Scott in his tracks, his face closing down. It wasn't the girl's fault. She didn't know what memories her words had just unleashed to strike him with an almost physical force. She had just turned an impulse into a stark reality. His return to Coorah Creek was no longer something in his future. It was here and now and he wasn't really ready for it. That wasn't a good sign. He struggled for a few seconds to regain an appearance of normality.

'No truck,' he said. 'I've got a rope in my car. I'll tow you in.'

'But I don't know . . . ' The girl's voice trailed off, and Scott saw the apprehension in her eyes. *You and me both*, he thought.

'Perhaps it would help if I introduced myself. I'm Scott Collins,' he said. 'And

I promise you I am not an axe murderer or even a car thief.'

That almost wiped the tension from her face. Her lips twitched in the start of a smile. 'Hi Scott. I'm Katie Brooks.'

She held out her hand and he took it briefly. Like Katie herself, it was small and looked far too delicate for life in the outback.

'I'll get the rope.'

3

Ed Collins didn't recognise either of the approaching cars. He squinted against the glare outside his workshop. He'd been Coorah Creek's only garage and mechanic for more than thirty years. There wasn't a car within 200 kilometres he hadn't worked on or filled with petrol. These must be tourists, passing through on their way to Birdsville. He studied the blue car. It was getting on in years. It wasn't surprising that it was being towed. He hoped the driver wasn't planning to take it into the desert. People died doing stupid things like that.

The car towing it was interesting. It looked like one of those hybrids. He'd read about them. Never seen one though. The Creek wasn't a place for flash environmentally friendly cars. Workhorses. That's what the cars out here were. It was too much to hope he'd get his hands on the car, but it would be nice to have a look under the bonnet. If the driver seemed a good bloke and was going to be around for a day or two, maybe he'd get a chance.

Ed picked up an old rag and began wiping his hands. The owner of a car like that wasn't going to want greasy handprints on his shiny new paint. As he tossed the rag aside, Ed looked at his hands. The dirt never really seemed to come off. Not that it mattered. There was no one he wanted to impress. He was a mechanic. Always had been and always would be. Mechanics had dirty hands. People just had to accept that.

The lead car angled off the road towards the garage and began to slow. Ed could see the person being towed wasn't paying attention. He knew what was going to happen next. The Commodore clipped the back of the hybrid, shunting it forward. Both drivers hit the brakes and the cars came to a halt about a metre apart.

A girl jumped out of the Commodore. She was young and blonde and pretty. And very distraught.

'Oh my God. I am so sorry!' As upset as she was, her English accent was still very pronounced. She bent over to examine the damage to the back of the hybrid.

'I wasn't paying attention. It's all my fault. I'll pay to get it fixed.'

So, maybe he would get to work on the hybrid after all. Ed stepped towards the open door, but stopped in shock as the driver of the hybrid got out of his car.

Eight years is a long time. In eight years, regret can eat at a man's soul leaving him empty and lonely. In eight years a boy becomes a man. But even after eight years, a father knows his own son.

Shocked to his core, Ed took half a step backward to remain hidden in the dim interior of his workshop.

His son . . . Scott . . . wasn't paying any attention to the girl. He was studying the outside of the garage. He wouldn't find anything changed, Ed thought. At least, not the building.

'I feel just so bad about this,' the girl was still apologising. 'After you rescued me when I was in trouble.'

'Don't worry about it.'

His voice was the same. So too was the shock of brown wavy hair. Just like Ed's when he was young. And the way he stood, straight and sure of himself. As a teenager, Scott had always been unwilling to back down or give an inch. It didn't look like that had changed.

But something must have changed, because he was here — in the place he had left, vowing never to return.

Ed's hands were shaking. He jammed them deep into the pockets of his dirty overalls. He had to do something. He couldn't just stand in the shadows looking at his son. But he wasn't ready to face him yet. He just needed another minute.

'I can't say how sorry I am, or how grateful.'

24

The girl was still talking. Ed wondered who she was. It sounded like she was a stranger Scott had found on the side of the road.

'Anyone would have done the same.' Scott finally turned his attention back to the girl. He dropped to the ground and reached under the Commodore to untie the tow rope.

Now was the time, Ed knew. He should go and speak to them. He wished the girl wasn't there. He would much rather have been alone when he faced his son for the first time after so many years. There was a lot they had to say to each other. Things that couldn't be said in front of a stranger. In front of anyone. But it looked like he wasn't going to get any choice.

He took a step forward.

Outside, he saw Scott stiffen, staring in Ed's direction. Had his son seen him?

'You'll be fine now,' Scott said to the girl, without taking his eyes from the door of the garage. Then he turned, quickly got back behind the wheel of his car. Within a few seconds he was gone.

His son didn't want to see him. Ed's heart was pounding. He wasn't sure what he felt. Relief at having more time to prepare for their meeting. Fear that Scott might leave town without ever talking to him. He wanted to know what had brought him back after so long. And most of all, he desperately needed to know if Scott had ever found what he was searching for.

Outside, the girl was still waiting.

Ed took a deep breath and walked out into the bright sunlight.

'G'day.'

'Hello. I'm afraid my car has broken down. Radiator, I think.'

'I'll take a look.'

Working on cars had always been Ed's great joy. Even at the worst of times, he could lose himself in his work and put his troubles to one side. Not so today. He took a cursory glance.

'Yeah. Radiator. It'll need replacing. I

can get one in for you. Take a couple of days though.'

'That's all right. I'm here to stay. I'm going to be working at the hospital. My name is Katie. Katie Brooks.'

'Ed.' There was no need to tell her more than that. 'Lucky for you that bloke was able to tow you in. Is he a friend of yours?'

'No. He found me on the side of the road. Good thing too. I was out of water and starting to worry.'

'A good bloke then?'

'Oh yes. He was just great!'

Ed looked at her face as she spoke. There was a shine in her eyes that told him his son had impressed this girl. Clearly she was hoping to see him again. Ed knew that look. A woman had once looked at him like that. A long time ago. It hadn't lasted long, but how sweet it had been. It had given him a son, but that relationship too had soured.

Ed felt just a small flare of hope deep inside. Maybe he was about to get a second chance.

4

Scott felt bad about leaving the poor girl so abruptly. He wasn't normally that rude. She seemed rather nice. She was also very pretty and just a little bit lost. It must be tough for someone so very English to find themselves all the way out here, beyond the black stump. He was normally more than happy to help a lady — especially one with blonde hair and blue eyes, but he'd had to get out of there. He did not want to face the man he'd seen moving in the shadows inside the garage.

He turned the corner and parked outside the pub. He switched his engine off and looked up at the two storey building. It hadn't changed. The paint looked fairly new. It hadn't faded or developed that faint powdery look caused by long exposure to the harsh outback sun. But it was the same colour he remembered. The lovely wrought iron railings still edged the balcony on the top floor, twisting in intricate lacework. He had always loved this old building. So beautiful and elegant. So different from the garage and the shabby house behind it.

Scott slowly got out of the car and turned to look about him. The pub might not have changed, but the rest of the town certainly had.

He remembered the general store, but it was larger now. Had it been extended? The feed store was still the same, but what was that across the road? A ladies' hair salon? That was new. So were the clothing store and the houses that he could see in the distance, either side of the town's other main road — the one that led north to Mount Isa. When he'd last seen Coorah Creek, the Goongalla Uranium Mine was just a topic of conversation and a hope for the future. Obviously the mine had prospered and the town along with it.

He was glad about that.

He turned around and walked the few steps back towards the T-intersection that was the heart of the town. He could see the garage now. Any prosperity brought by the mine hadn't touched that. It was still shabby and dirty. Even more so than he remembered. It occupied the corner opposite the pub. From this angle, he could see the workshop and the petrol bowsers. Eight years had passed since he'd last seen it and to his eyes it looked exactly the same. Nothing had changed. It didn't even appear to have benefited from a new coat of paint in all that time. Over the top of the rusting tin workshop roof, he could see gum trees reaching skywards. That would be the garden around the house. He remembered those trees, but they had been a lot smaller back then.

Katie's car was still sitting outside the workshop. The bonnet was up, but he could see no sign of either its driver or the man who was fixing it. She would be all right, he thought. The old man was honest and would easily repair her radiator. And he'd charge a fair price for the work. No-one had ever accused the old man of doing wrong by a customer. His family though . . .

Scott went back to his car. At some point he was going to have to enquire about a room at the pub, but not right now. Since he had driven past the town sign, memories had been flooding back. Among those memories was the publican's wife — a garrulous woman with a real taste for gossip. If he checked into the hotel now, the whole town would know he was here in just five minutes.

He wasn't ready for that yet.

He slid back behind the wheel of his car and pulled away from the pub. He'd drive around for a while, just to have a look at the town.

It didn't take long. The town might have grown a lot in eight years, but it still wasn't very big. The houses on the north side all looked fairly new. They must have come with the mine, he thought. The old police station was still there, but it was now part of some kind of town square. The school was bigger than in his day. And it had a swimming pool! Now that was an improvement. Curious, he drove towards the southern side of town where he knew the mine must be. He wouldn't mind taking a look at it. A couple of miles out of town, a good quality bitumen road led off to the left. He turned down it and sure enough, there were the gates to the mine. He drove straight past, following the chain link fence until he came to . . . an airport? Things certainly had changed.

But now he had run out of excuses. Reluctantly he executed a three point turn on the narrow road and drove back in the direction of town.

There she was again. Standing in the middle of the road. What was with this girl?

Scott pulled up next to her.

'Katie? Is everything all right?' Surely nothing had happened at the garage to send her running away?

'Oh, hello Scott.' The girl seemed pleased to see him. 'I'm heading for the hospital, which I'm told is just down this road.'

'The hospital?' Scott's first thought was since when had Coorah Creek boasted a hospital? His second was — why was she looking for a doctor? Surely the old man . . .

'Are you all right?' he asked.

'Yes,' she said. A small frown creased her forehead, and then faded as she suddenly grinned. 'No. No. I'm fine. I'm going to work there.'

'Of course, you said you were a nurse.'

'That's right. One who should have known enough about heat stroke and dehydration to carry water.' As she spoke, she raised her hand. There was a new, large and almost full bottle of water in it. 'Anyway Ed, I think that was his name . . . the man at the garage . . . said it was a short walk down here to the hospital. I'm expected. So I thought I would walk.'

Scott felt a small surge of relief. If she couldn't remember the mechanic's name, then she had definitely not made the connection between them. But no doubt she would in the not too distant future.

'I passed what I think may be the hospital just back there a bit,' Scott said. 'I'll give you a lift. It's far too hot to walk.'

He felt her hesitation. She was feeling a bit lost. A long way from home. He understood how that felt.

'Get in,' he said. 'I've already towed you in from the highway, what does another half a mile matter?'

Her smile was very appealing. Slightly crooked, but it lit her blue eyes as well.

'Thank you,' she said as she slid into the passenger's seat. 'You're right. It is far too hot to walk. I've had more than enough sun for one day.'

He cast a sideways glance at her. Her fair skin was already looking far too pink. He hoped she would be careful. The outback sun would be tough on her. And maybe not just the sun . . .

'So why Coorah Creek?' he asked as he turned the car again.

'I came to Australia for a working holiday,' she said. 'I was so sick of the cold weather and the rain. This was the first job I found.'

'You won't have any problem with cold wet weather here,' Scott said as he slipped the car back into gear.

* * *

Katie had to agree with him. She had never been so hot in all her life. Not even on that holiday in Spain. She was drenched with sweat just from walking a short distance from the garage where her car was being worked on by the shabby mechanic. Her feet hurt, because open-toed sandals were just not the right footwear for a place like this. Her skin felt flushed and burnt, and she was about to meet her new boss. Or at least, that was what she was expecting to do. She had e-mailed him to let him know to expect her this afternoon. But so far very little of this trip had turned out the way she planned it.

She hadn't seen much of Coorah Creek, but what she had seen wasn't quite what she'd had in mind. It was so small! And very quiet. Dry as well as hot. Most of the houses she'd seen were very old and shabby and rather than the red brick of her homeland, they were made of wood. The centre of the town, if that was what it could be called, was tiny, with just a handful of shops. It was such a long long way from Oxford Street and there were certainly no Christmas lights to be seen. The shops did look a bit more prosperous than the garage. That made her hope that her first impressions might be wrong.

Scott, however, had been a pleasant surprise. She cast a quick sideways glance at him. He looked to be in his mid-twenties. About the same age as her. He had a kind face. Not exactly handsome, but not unattractive. His hair was non-descript brown. His eyes were non-descript brown. His skin was tanned, and the hands gripping the steering wheel looked strong and competent. She liked that. The way he had dashed off after dropping her at the garage was a bit disconcerting. He must have had a reason. Some secret perhaps that he didn't want to share. There was nothing wrong with that, of course. Everyone had secrets. She certainly did.

Scott had been there when she needed help and he seemed really nice. She wasn't entirely comfortable alone in the car with a stranger, but she did feel a little bad about lying to him just now. Adventure had very little to do with her reasons for being here. But two accidental meetings weren't enough to encourage the exchange of her secrets either.

Katie's heart shrank a little when Scott turned into a driveway next to a painted wooden sign that identified the Coorah Creek Hospital. The building ahead of them didn't look like any hospital she had ever seen. For a start, it was built of wood. No brick or stone edifice of the type she was used to back in England, this hospital was a long low building built on wooden stumps and surrounded by a deep veranda. She had expected it to be small — but it looked barely big enough to accommodate a handful of patients.

As Scott pulled up near the broad front stairs, a young couple emerged. The girl was carrying a toddler in her arms. She looked far too young to be its mother. Katie smiled at them as she got out of the car.

'Hello,' the young mother said. 'I bet you're the new nurse. Doctor Adam told us you were coming today. We've been waiting for you. I'm Nikki and this is my boyfriend Steve.'

'Oh,' Katie tried not to seem surprised by this. 'Is the doctor here?'

'He was,' the young man replied. 'He and Jess had to go. They've flown up to the Isa with an injured miner.'

Katie struggled with this latest information. She knew there was an air ambulance operating out of Coorah Creek. Her new job would include flying in that air ambulance as they tended to patients on outlying stations. Perhaps Jess was the pilot. As for 'the Isa' . . . she had no idea. There were times she felt as if the Australians didn't speak English at all, but rather some entirely different language.

'Doctor Adam asked us to meet you and show you to your place,' Nikki said.

'All right.' Katie wasn't entirely sure that it was all right, but it appeared that once again she didn't have a lot of choice.

'Right. This way.' Steve turned back into the hospital. Katie paused for a moment and turned back towards the car, where Scott was standing next to the open driver's side door. Obviously he was eager to leave. She didn't blame him. He probably had better things to do with his time than act as her chauffeur.

'Scott. Thanks for rescuing me . . . again.'

'You are very welcome.' He mimed tipping his hat in her direction and slid back behind the wheel.

As he drove away, Katie felt suddenly bereft. He was the closest thing she had to a friend for several thousand miles, and he was leaving her. She shook her head. Jet lag, she thought. And exhaustion. And the heat. She'd soon find her feet.

She followed the young couple into the hospital. The moment she stepped into the shade of the veranda, she felt the temperature drop. The building was surprisingly cool, despite the lack of air conditioning.

'You don't have any bags,' Steve said.

'They're in the back of my car,' Katie told him. 'It broke down just out of town. It's at the garage getting fixed.'

'I'm sure someone will run them over for you.'

This town must be full of good Samaritans and knights in shining armour, she thought.

'These used to be Doctor Adam's

rooms. Before he and Jess got married,' Nikki said as she led the way down a hallway and opened the very last door.

The rooms in question were near the rear of the hospital. Katie stepped into a big living room. There was a small dining table and a big armchair. Empty bookshelves lined one wall. She assumed the doors opposite led to a bedroom and bathroom — at least, she hoped that's where they led. She could see a small kitchen through an open doorway to her left.

'We have to go now,' Nikki said. 'Doctor Adam and Jess will be back in a couple of hours. You'll like them. They delivered Anna together.' She kissed her child's head, and the young man beside her almost glowed with pleasure as she did.

Katie watched them leave, her head in a spin. She closed the door behind them and leaned back against it. The sheer emptiness of her new living quarters suddenly crashed down on her like a ton of rocks. She was a million miles from home, hot and dirty and exhausted.

She was about to spend Christmas without her family for the very first time and she doubted there was so much as a kettle and cup in the kitchen for making a cup of tea. To top it all off, she was a nurse in a place where — the girl's words suddenly sank in — a pilot helped to deliver a baby.

She had gambled her whole future on this job. Had she made a terrible mistake?

5

Pub or garage? Scott was pretty certain he didn't want to go into either. He'd really rather go back to the hospital and spend some more time with Katie. At least she had seemed happy to see him. And her smile was a far more pleasant prospect than what awaited him.

Garage or pub?

He pulled his car up in front of the pub. Through the windows, he could see someone moving around in the bar. In his rear view mirror, he could see the garage. No sign of movement there.

There really wasn't any choice. He'd been an angry teenager when he'd stormed out of Coorah Creek, but there were people who would remember him. The publican's wife was one of them. She had good reason to remember him. He winced slightly at the memory. If he walked into the pub, news of his return would fly through Coorah Creek like a storm.

He had to go to the garage and face what was waiting for him there before word of his return made matters a whole lot worse.

It took a lot of willpower to reach for the door handle.

He crossed the street, but instead of walking into the garage, his steps took him a little further to a side gate that led directly to the house next door. Between the scrubby bushes, he could see that his old home had changed; become poorer and more ill kept, with its peeling paint and rusty tin roof. The gate was rusty too. He did not move to open it.

A dog barked.

Scott searched the unkempt garden as the animal barked again. It was a rough, weak sound. Surely not . . .

The Labrador came into view. She was moving slowly and limping a little, pausing every few seconds to bark in Scott's general direction. She was old.

So very old. Finally she arrived at the gate and stared up at him through rheumy eyes.

'Candy, old friend. Do you remember me?' Scott dropped to a crouch and reached his hand through the bars of the gate. The dog lifted her head as if to bark, and then hesitated. She lowered her nose to sniff Scott's outstretched fingers. Slowly her tail began to wag and she licked his hand.

Scott felt tears prick his eyes. His few good memories of Coorah Creek all seemed to involve his dog. Abandoned as a boisterous half-grown pup by some passing vehicle, she had come into a lonely boy's life and made it just that little bit less lonely. She had loved him — unconditionally as dogs do. And he had loved her back because there was no-one else to love. Leaving her behind when he left had almost broken him. But taking her had been impossible.

He'd never expected Candy to still be here. To still be alive after all these years. Her eyes were foggy and her muzzle was almost completely grey, but for such an old dog, she looked quite well. She'd obviously been cared for.

And she remembered him.

'So, are you just here to see the dog, or were you planning to come to the house?'

Scott closed his eyes for a few seconds, as if by doing so he could still avoid this confrontation. The familiar voice was not as strong as it had once been. But the anger was still there. And he felt an answering echo of anger in his own heart. Some things that he had hoped might change obviously had not. Slowly he got to his feet.

The man standing in front of him had aged too. His hair was grey and his skin dry and wrinkled after years of exposure to the harsh outback sun. Ed Collins was fifty, but he looked more like sixty. His eyes, though, had not changed. Not one bit. They were still hard.

'Hello, Dad.' It seemed such a banal thing to say, but he could think of nothing else.

'So, you're back then?'

Not for long, Scott thought. In fact, right now he wanted nothing more than to just get in his car and drive away. But he'd come all this way with a purpose. He couldn't leave without at least trying.

'It's been a long time,' he said.

His father said nothing. The old man was staring at him, his face fixed and unreadable. Scott knew that look. He also knew that his father's hands would be clenched into fists. He had strong hands, permanently stained with grease and oil. Large strong hands and powerful fists.

This was so much harder than Scott had thought. The memories were tumbling around in his mind. Memories that time had faded to black and white were flaring in brilliant colour, and the pain was as real as it had been all those years ago. He felt seventeen again.

Sitting between them Candy whined. Maybe the old dog remembered this too . . . father and son facing each other down. The air full of anger.

'Did you ever find her?'

After more than eight years, this was all his father had to ask him. Not how are you son? Or what have you done with your life? Not even if he was married or had a family. The bitterness was so strong Scott could taste it.

He shook his head as he turned away.

'No.' He didn't care if his father heard the answer or not.

He was walking away again. This time he didn't have the excuse of youth and anger, but that didn't matter. The desire to get away from that house and his father was equally as strong. And now, as then, he really didn't have any place to go, so once again he walked across the road and into the pub.

The first thing he saw was the tree. He could hardly miss it — covered as it was with flashing lights and tinsel and shining balls of red and silver. Christmas. He'd forgotten all about it. Not that Christmas had meant much to him for a very long time. Not since the day his mother walked out of the house behind the garage. He'd been just eleven years old. The next few years had been dark and unhappy — until the day a seventeen year old boy and his father had traded blows — and he'd walked away.

His fists still tingled with the memory.

The holiday meant nothing to him except a chance to earn double time at the various jobs he'd held. He'd never planned to come back at Christmas. He'd never planned to come back . . . ever. But plans change.

'G'day. What can I get you?' The man behind the bar was a few years older than Scott. He was unfamiliar. Perhaps the elderly couple he remembered had sold the pub and moved on.

'Beer thanks.'

Scott sat down on a bar stool. He was the only patron in the pub — not surprising as it was barely five o'clock. If someone had asked him to describe this place yesterday, he would have said he didn't really remember. But now that he was here, he remembered it all. The long polished wooden bar. The big windows open to catch any hint of breeze. The fans turning slowly overhead because there never was any breeze. The glasses neatly lined up on shelves behind the bar were also there in his memory.

'Well, look who we have here. Scott Collins. I wasn't expecting to ever see you sitting at my bar again.'

He remembered the woman who had just entered the bar. Her face was a little more lined and her hair a lot more grey. But her eyes were alive with interest.

'Hello Mrs Warren.'

'It's been what — seven or eight years?' Her smile was tentative. 'Hopefully this visit will be a better one than last time you were here.'

'Well, better for me. I got my beer this time.'

'This time you're not seventeen.'

Or fighting mad, he wanted to add. Mrs Warren had refused to serve him that day when he'd stormed in here nursing bruised knuckles and looking for a ride out of town.

'It's a bit late, but I'd like to apologise for the window, Mrs Warren.'

'Apology accepted,' Mrs Warren moved behind the bar. 'Just don't do it again. Your father covered the damage last time. I don't imagine he'd do it a second time.'

His father had paid for the broken window? That was unexpected.

'So, you're back for Christmas then?'

The woman he remembered was always on the lookout for some juicy gossip, and he was afraid he was going to be the subject of that gossip whatever he said or did.

'I need a room,' he said, avoiding the question.

'We have rooms,' Mrs Warren replied. 'The pub is pretty much empty now. Not many people come out here at Christmas. More likely to head east to the coast. I've never been one for the coast, mind. I don't like swimming in the sea. And I'm too old now to be a beach bunny.'

Trish Warren had always talked a lot. That certainly hadn't changed.

'I can pay up front if you like,' Scott said. 'As I have a bad record with you.'

There was no answer. Scott found himself being scrutinised by a pair of very sharp eyes. Mrs Warren gave him a very thorough once over before looking him straight in the face. He held her gaze for a few seconds, then she nodded, as if making up her mind about something.

'That's all right,' she said as the phone at the end of the bar suddenly rang. 'I guess I can trust you.'

'Thanks Mrs Warren.'

'You'd better start calling me Trish.'

While Trish answered the phone, Scott looked down at the beer in his hands. He could still see the small scar on his forearm from the last time he'd entered this bar. Mrs Warren — he would never have called her Trish back then — had refused to serve him a beer because he was underage. He'd just stormed out of his father's house, laden down with a rucksack with all his possessions and a whole heap of anger. He stormed out of the pub too, but on the way he had put his fist through a window. Only some remarkably good luck had saved him from doing permanent damage to himself.

And his father had paid for the window. Scott wasn't quite sure what to make of that.

Trish's voice dragged him out of his reverie. She had hung up the phone and was now talking to the barman he'd seen earlier.

' . . . at the hospital by herself. Adam needs someone to go over there.'

'It that Katie you're talking about?' he asked.

'Yes. The new nurse.' Trish's eyes narrowed. 'I hear she got towed into town by a stranger today after her car broke down. I guess that was you, wasn't it?'

'I guess so.' He would be a stranger to most of the residents. 'I dropped her at the hospital to wait for the doctor.'

'That was him on the phone. He's not going to get back tonight. He wanted someone to tell her and make sure she was all right. Jack can run over . . . '

'I'll do it,' Scott interrupted her.

Trish turned and raised an eyebrow. He knew why. The kid he'd once been hadn't been one for offering a helping hand.

'It'll be better if I do it. She knows me,' he explained. 'Or at least, she's met me. A familiar face might help. She's probably feeling a little lost and maybe a little scared.'

He knew only too well how that felt.

To his surprise, Trish nodded.

'You're probably right. But just stay there and finish your beer. I'll give you some food to take over for her. I know Jess — that's the doctor's wife — stocked the fridge in the flat, but it'll be easier if I send something over she can just re-heat.

There'll be enough for two, if she wants you to keep her company.'

'All right. Thanks.'

'Don't get too carried away.' Trish smiled. 'I never got you to pay for that broken window, but you will be paying for dinner for two tonight.'

6

It was too quiet. The silence was almost a physical thing. Katie stood on the steps of the hospital and gazed out into the deepening twilight. In the west, the sun was very low on the horizon, a ball of molten gold beneath a sky totally devoid of any clouds. The brilliant blue sky of the afternoon was slowly turning a deep royal blue as the first stars began to appear — like diamonds on soft velvet. It was quite beautiful and unlike any sunset she had ever seen before.

But it was so very very quiet.

She was a girl from London. The city was always full of sound. The rumble of cars, or buses or trains. At any hour of the night or day, you could hear people. The voices of late night travellers. Televisions in living rooms or music floating through an open window. There were dogs barking and street lights. In

London you were never alone. There were thousands — millions — of people close by, and at times it felt as if it was a battle just to have enough space to breathe.

But out here, she was terrifyingly alone.

From where she stood, she couldn't see any other houses with lights. In fact, she couldn't see any other houses at all. She might have been the only person left on the planet. She knew the road was just a short distance away, but there were no cars. There were no voices . . . just . . . she stopped and listened. Suddenly the night was not as silent as she'd thought. There were noises. Creaks and groans from the building behind her. A sudden rustling of leaves in the big gum tree by the car park. The screech of some sort of bird. It was all so alien. How she longed for the comforting rumble of an Underground train.

Casting a nervous glance over her shoulder, Katie walked back into the hospital. That was no better. The hospital was as empty and as strange as the rest of Coorah Creek. There were no patients in the rooms. No other staff. No nurses hurrying about their work, or doctors doing their rounds. There was just her.

A few weeks ago, she would have welcomed the peace. All her life, the only thing she had ever wanted was to be a nurse. To help people. But the reality of her job was not what she expected. She loved the work and caring for her patients brought her enormous satisfaction. Helping someone through a difficult time was a source of joy, and her recent move into A&E nursing had been a reward for a lot of very hard work. Day after day, the long hours left her teetering on the edge of exhaustion, but that wasn't the part that had so nearly destroyed her calling.

As a student nurse, it had not occurred to her that a hospital would be a seething bed of rivalries and politics and unspoken rules. She had withered under restriction, both official and unwritten, that had sometimes prevented her doing what her heart told her she should. She hated the doctors who seemed to consider the nurses as some sort of private harem. And equally she hated the doctors who treated the nurses as if they were nothing more than servants. This wasn't the medicine she wanted to practice, but in the great overstretched bureaucracy that was the National Health Service, it was the only medicine she seemed likely to ever know.

After one particularly long and fraught shift that lasted almost twenty-four hours, she had looked around and realised her heart was no longer in her job. She was dragging her feet each day as she made her way to work on the Underground. She had to make a change.

This job at a small outback hospital had seemed the answer to a prayer — a chance to get away from the daily grind of a big London hospital. It was a chance to get away from the long hours and the exhaustion and be able to give more than a few moments to help each person. She wanted to answer a call for assistance as soon as she heard it, and not to have to put one person ahead of another. In a smaller community, she could really make a difference. She hoped that here in this small town, she could recapture her love of her job. She would be working with an air ambulance too. That sounded amazing. Not to mention the excitement and adventure of living in the Australian outback. It hadn't taken her long to get her paperwork in order and book a flight.

It had all sounded perfect — but looking around her now — Katie was starting to wonder if she'd been terribly wrong to come here.

The only lights were in the hallway and in her flat at the rear of the building. The glass doors swung shut behind her. Should she lock them? It didn't seem right to lock the door to a hospital, but if she was the only one there, what was to stop anyone just walking in and stealing something? Or . . . worse. She examined the door. There didn't seem to be any sort of lock. That settled that, but she would be sure to lock the door to her flat.

She couldn't do that either. When she walked back into her quarters, she discovered her door had no lock either. Did no-one in this town ever lock their doors?

Feeling bewildered and a little bit anxious, Katie walked over to the television and turned it on. The sound of voices filled the empty space around her. That helped, but it did not completely chase away her restlessness.

It was probably jet lag, she decided. She suddenly realised she was hungry. She hadn't eaten since that sandwich in her car several hours and many many miles ago. She had already discovered that her small kitchen was well stocked with essentials — tea, milk and even some home baked biscuits. But she needed something a bit more substantial than that. She took another look in the fridge and the cupboards. She could probably manage some scrambled eggs. Not quite what her rumbling stomach was after, but she didn't have a lot of choice. Her car was still at the garage and she wasn't going to walk out into the night in search of a grocery store. She wasn't a coward, but neither was she stupid. She had no idea who or what might be out there in the darkness here on the edge of nowhere.

Just as she was about to sink into a bottomless chasm of self-pity, she saw a flash of light through her window. A car had just pulled into the hospital car park.

As Katie walked down the corridor towards the hospital's front door, she was beginning to wish she had something in her hands. Something like a cricket bat. But, she chided herself, this was a hospital and she was a nurse. This was more likely to be someone in need of medical help than a murderer.

The glass doors opened and the only familiar face for a thousand miles . . . or kilometres . . . smiled at her.

'Hi Katie. We have got to stop meeting like this.'

'Scott!' Her heart slowed its nervous pounding, but not completely. 'I am beginning to wonder if you are the only other person in Coorah Creek,' she joked, hiding her relief.

'Actually, I don't live here,' the laughter in his voice faded. 'I'm just . . . visiting for a while.'

Katie wondered how long 'a while' might be. Scott was the closest thing she had to a friend, and she wasn't ready to lose him yet.

He was also, she suddenly thought, a very attractive man. Her first impressions earlier that day had been so very wrong. His brown eyes were deep and dark — with a dash of gold. She could get lost in those eyes. His brown hair curled in a way designed to make a girl just want to run her fingers through it. He was tall, with a lean, hard body and his skin was tanned a lovely golden colour. How had she thought him non-descript? His arms looked very strong. Looked like they would feel good wrapped around her. When his eyes met hers, she felt as if she was the only person in the world he was thinking about.

Katie felt her face starting to colour. What was she thinking? It must be the jet lag. Or exhaustion. Or loneliness. She didn't normally get all lustful on the third date — except, it wasn't their third date. Their meetings had been accidents, not dates, even though each time Scott appeared, her heart had given an excited little thump. And besides, a girl couldn't be blamed for feeling . . . kindly . . . towards the man who had rescued her twice.

'So, why have you come to the hospital?' Katie reached deep inside herself and found the nurse. 'Have you hurt yourself?'

'No. I come bearing messages and food.'

For the first time, Katie noticed the carrier bag. It was bulging. And there was the faintest smell of food in the air. Her stomach rumbled very loudly.

'Well, I guess that means I came at the right time,' Scott laughed.

Katie blushed and tried to cover her embarrassment by leading Scott down the hallway towards her flat. Once inside, he placed the bag on the table.

'Trish Warren over at the pub sent this over. There's some sort of lamb and potato stew. I hope you're not vegetarian.'

'No, I'm not. Lamb stew sounds good,' Katie said. 'What was the message?'

'The doctor apparently flew to The Isa today with a patient and they are not going to make it back tonight. He rang the pub and asked Trish to make sure you were all right. That you were settled in and had food and stuff. Oh, he sends his apologies too and says he will see you tomorrow morning.'

The news didn't come as much of a surprise to Katie. She had no real idea where 'The Isa' might be, but after hearing the news of the evacuation flight earlier, she had already begun to suspect the doctor wasn't returning today.

'Why didn't he ring me here?' she wondered out loud.

'Apparently your phone was disconnected when the doctor moved out and hasn't been fixed yet. He rang the pub because that's pretty much the centre of the town. He knew someone there would be able to get a message to you.'

'This is the first time I have made it to a job interview and the boss hasn't,' Katie joked.

'But haven't you already got the job? Surely you didn't come all this way just for an interview?'

'I've got the job. But it's sort of a provisional thing. Three months' probation. If I don't like it — or they don't like me . . . '

'I'm sure they'll love you.' His words seemed genuine as did the smile that curved his lips.

'Well, thanks for telling me. And

bringing the food,' she said, trying to hide the fact that she was blushing again.

'You are welcome.'

He showed no sign of leaving. Not that Katie wanted him to leave. It felt good not to be alone. But there was the matter of dinner. Her stomach rumbled again.

'You need to eat,' Scott said. He hesitated a moment before adding, 'Trish has put enough in there to feed a small army. And I put in a couple of beers. Just in case you felt like company. It doesn't seem right that you should spend your first night in town all alone. But if you'd rather I left, that's okay too. I can easily go back . . . '

'No,' Katie broke in before he'd finished speaking. 'Stay. Please. I'd enjoy some company.'

A few minutes later, they were seated around her small table, steaming food dished out on plates, and beer bottles dripping condensation onto the wood.

'So,' Scott said between mouthfuls,

'tell me more about what brought you all the way from England to Coorah Creek.'

'I was looking for adventure,' she told him. 'But this job also sounded pretty amazing. I'll be working with an Air Ambulance. Doesn't that sound great?'

The conversation flowed freely, but neither of them allowed it to become too personal. Instead, she and Scott spent the evening sharing anecdotes, talking about books and films and music.

And laughing.

And keeping a promise Katie had made to herself as her plane had risen through the grey clouds above London's Heathrow Airport. She had stared out the glass window of the jet and vowed that as soon as she arrived in her new home, she would have dinner with a handsome man to drive away any homesickness and doubt.

On this first night in Coorah Creek — she did just that.

And Scott did his part too.

7

In the early morning light, Coorah Creek looked almost . . . nice. The gentle wash of dawn colour softened the harsh red of the dry earth to mellow amber. The dusty blue-grey gum trees appeared fresh and green. And as the stars faded, the arc above him was a pleasing royal blue — not the blinding hard blue of midday.

Ed was always up early. This morning, though, he had been awake much earlier than usual. To be honest, he hadn't slept a great deal. After the girl left yesterday, he'd hoped against hope he would see the silver grey hybrid heading back towards the garage. That hadn't happened. Later, during the evening, he'd considered going to the pub. If Scott was still in town, that's where he'd stay. There was nowhere else.

Convincing himself that he was taking the dog for a walk, he'd crossed the road and strolled past the pub. Slowly, because Candy was an old dog and couldn't walk too fast. There had been no sign of Scott's car. Ed occasionally visited the pub, when he felt the need for human company. Trish was always willing to talk, even if he rarely answered. She served a good steak too. But Ed was in no mood for her gossip. He did not want to learn about his son from her. He'd returned to the quiet dark house behind the garage, and spent the evening with the dog at his side, trying not to listen for the sound of a car pulling up outside his home.

This morning, he'd given up the pretence. Letting Candy out to do her business, Ed had then walked through the rusty gate and stared across at the pub. Mentally, he checked off each of the half dozen cars he could see parked nearby. There was no hybrid.

Ed's heart sank just a little. Had

Scott left? Their encounter yesterday had been as harsh as it had been brief. Maybe too harsh, but he was still struggling to come to terms with seeing his son again. Ed was suddenly afraid that he had driven Scott away for the second time.

He felt a gentle nudge against his leg, and bent slightly to pat Candy's head. The old dog waved her tail slowly.

'You want to see him again too, don't you girl?'

Candy barked softly.

'I know.' Ed turned back towards the house. As he was up, he might as well get a cup of coffee and get to work. He had a couple of cars in the shop right now as well as that girl's radiator to replace. He might as well open the garage early, just in case Scott was still in town and wanted to see him.

'Come on Candy. Time for breakfast old girl.'

The dog barked again, but didn't leave the gate.

'Candy. Come on.'

71

Still the dog didn't move. The road outside was deserted. There was nothing to be barking at. Shaking his head, Ed climbed the stairs into the house. The dog was getting old and senile. She would come when she was ready.

* * *

As Scott drove slowly back towards the pub, he glanced over at the house but saw no movement. It was still very early. He assumed the old man wasn't awake yet. He was glad. He just wasn't ready to talk to his father again. He'd spent such an enjoyable time with Katie last night, he didn't want anything to spoil his mood. He had not intended to stay the night at the hospital, but he and Katie had talked over dinner and on into the small hours of this morning. Talked easily and enjoyably about so many things. He couldn't for the life of him remember everything they talked about. But the sound of her laugh — that he could remember. They had drunk his two cans of beer and many cups of coffee until finally, Katie had yawned her way to bed. Scott had spent the few remaining hours of darkness sleeping on the couch, explaining to Katie that the pub was likely to be locked, and he might not get in to his room.

What he didn't explain to her was the other reason he'd stayed. He'd seen the nervousness and loneliness in her eyes and her relief when she realised it was him at the hospital doors. No-one knew better than he how hard it could be leaving home for the first time and being all alone in a new place. He'd been a teenager when he left . . . ran away . . and knew just how scary the wide world could be if there was no one standing beside you. He was a grown man now, yet there were times, and this was one of them, when he didn't want to be alone either. And if he could help ease Katie's way at the same time, he would. Just out of kindness that was in no way related to her blue eyes, or the way she had smiled up at him from under her long blonde fringe.

But oh, she *was* pretty. And not a little bit sexy under that sweet face. Not that it mattered. He was just passing through. It wouldn't be fair to take advantage of her vulnerability. He would never do anything to hurt a woman. He was a very different man to his father. He'd just help Katie through these first few days, if she needed help.

He had left before she woke, starting the car as quietly as he could, fearful of waking her. His errant mind composed a picture of her asleep; her hair falling over her face, her body curled in such a way that a man could wrap his body around her and hold her while she slept. Or wake her . . .

Scott shook his head. He was not going to go there! This was the wrong time to be giving any woman a second thought, even if such second thoughts were very very appealing.

He parked the car outside the pub and looked across at his father's garage. The sun was a little higher in the sky now, any residual softness burned away by the rising heat and glare. The light was not flattering. There was nothing about the garage that looked in any way welcoming or homely. The pub seemed so much better right now.

'Good morning!'

Trish Warren was standing by the pub's open door.

'Good morning,' he said. His mind raced trying to think of how to explain his absence the night before. Not that he had to answer to anyone, but he would not want Mrs Warren — Trish — to start gossiping about Katie. That wouldn't be fair. 'By the time I had delivered Katie's dinner . . . Well . . . We talked and it got late. I wasn't sure if your door would be locked, so I slept on her couch.' He put a little extra emphasis on the last word.

'Careful there.' Trish's husband Syd appeared at her side. 'Trish will have you married off before you know what's going on.' The older man smiled at his wife with obvious affection, and much to Scott's surprise Trish almost blushed. She slapped her husband's arm gently.

'Get out of it,' she said. 'I'm just cooking breakfast, Scott. You'd best come and get some. There's nothing more important than a good breakfast to start a busy day. And I'm sure yours will be busy, as you've just come home after so many years.'

'Yes, Ma'am.'

Scott lingered over the well-cooked bacon and eggs and coffee Trish served. He lingered even longer over a hot shower. He even tidied his room before stepping out onto the wide veranda that enclosed the top floor of the hotel. From there, he could see across the street to the garage, which was now open. Somewhere in the shadowy recess of the workshop, his father would probably be bent over Katie's car. He felt a twinge of guilt that he hadn't told Katie that the grim old man at the garage was his father. She'd find out soon enough on the flourishing grapevine of Coorah Creek gossip.

In the meantime, he had come back

to the Creek with a purpose. Standing here was not going to get that accomplished.

He found his father removing the radiator from Katie's car.

'Is it bad?' he asked.

At the sound of Scott's voice, his father's hands stilled for a few seconds, but he didn't look up. Then he continued his work. 'It needs a new radiator. I've got one coming on the train on Wednesday.'

'Okay.'

The dimly lit workshop was silent except for the sound of Ed Collins working.

Scott looked around him. Nothing had changed here in the past eight years. The workshop was still littered with tools and engine parts and spare car wheels in a sort of semi-controlled chaos that only his father understood.

'She'll need her things.'

'What?'

'I said she'll need her things. That girl. The new nurse. You seem friendly with her. You could take them over to the hospital.'

His father was asking for his help? Well, not exactly asking; but it was something. 'All right. I'll get my car.'

Scott stepped back into the sunshine, feeling as if he had just taken a first very small step in achieving his goal. And the thought of seeing Katie again was icing on the cake. It was the work of just a few minutes to return to the pub and collect his car. When he returned, there was another car parked at the garage and a tall, dark-haired man was talking to his father. They both turned as he walked into the workshop.

'Adam, this is my son, Scott. Scott, this is Adam Gilmore. The doctor.'

Scott took the man's outstretched hand, trying not to show his shock at hearing the words 'my son' for the first time in so many years. Instead, he tried to focus on the man who must be Katie's boss. He had a firm grip and was as casually dressed as you would expect in a place like Coorah Creek.

Scott guessed he'd be considered handsome by some women. Would Katie think that?

'Thanks for helping out yesterday,' Adam said. 'I had planned to be here to meet Katie, but . . . well . . . the life of a doctor. You know how it is.'

'Glad to help,' Scott said.

'Anyway, we just flew back into town. I thought I would pick up her things and take them over to her by way of apology.'

There was nothing to say to that. Scott helped him load Katie's things into his car and watched him drive away. His father had returned to the workshop, his head once again buried under the bonnet of Katie's car. Scott really wasn't sure what to do. Maybe he'd taken a step in the right direction, but there was still a long way to go. He decided to head back to the pub and make use of the Wi-Fi there. He had a feeling he was going to stay in Coorah Creek longer than just a few days. There were some travel plans he needed to change.

8

There was no choice. She was going to have to walk back to the garage and collect her things. Katie rinsed her mouth out with water and looked down at her rumpled clothing. She looked like she had been dragged through a hedge backwards. Sometime today she was probably going to meet her new boss and this was not how she wanted to look when that happened. When she'd left her car at the garage yesterday, she had been too exhausted to think straight. And she had expected to be able to return for her things. It hadn't worked out quite like that. She wanted a change of clothes, some face cream and most of all, she wanted her toothbrush!

Katie avoided even glancing at the couch where Scott had spent the night. He'd been gone before she woke. She certainly didn't want him to see her looking like this, but if he'd still been here, she could have asked him to drive her back to the garage to pick her things up. That would have been a lot easier than walking.

She wasn't entirely sure how she felt about last night.

Scott being there had certainly eased her first night and driven away any fear or loneliness. The food and beer had been good. Not only that, Scott had actually listened to her when she talked and treated her like a real person. She hadn't had a man do that for a very long time. The only men in her recent past were the doctors at her hospital, who seemed to think that the nurses were simply there to serve them . . . in more ways than one.

Scott was different. When he looked at her he saw *her*, not just a nurse. And when she looked at him, she felt the occasional flutter in her stomach. She didn't believe in love at first sight, of course, but was such a thing as like at first sight? Like a lot . . .

She left the flat and walked through the hospital, hearing her footsteps echo in the empty hallway. It was a sound she had never before heard in a hospital. She stopped when she reached the hospital veranda. There was no lock on the door . . . should she just leave it? And was it right to leave the hospital totally unattended? What if someone needed help? Or broke in trying to steal drugs?

Even as the thought formed, a car appeared at the hospital gates. A small cloud of dust followed behind as it drove up and parked just a few yards away. A man got out and approached her.

'You must be Katie. Sorry about all this. I'm Adam Gilmore.'

On no! She took her boss's outstretched hand, mentally listing all the ways in which this was NOT going to be the best job interview she'd ever had.

'Dr Gilmore. I . . . I . . . Um . . . '

'Call me Adam. We're all very casual out here.'

'Um. Thank you Dr . . . Adam.'

'I'm sorry you were stranded last night, but we had to fly to the Isa. And I hear you had car trouble too. Ed Collins will soon get that fixed. But still, I guess it wasn't the best welcome to town. But if it helps, I've brought your things from the car.'

If it helps? How could it not help?

'Oh, that's really good of you . . . Adam. Thank you.'

The doctor turned back to the car and began pulling her bags from the back seat. Too late Katie realised that he'd brought everything from her car, including the empty water bottle and the loose shoes she had strewn across the back seat.

'Perhaps you'd better take these.' Adam was holding up a couple of shopping bags containing a swimming costume and some flip-flops that she'd bought the day she'd left Brisbane and headed for the outback.

She almost snatched them from his hand.

'I hope you're comfortable in the flat,' Adam said as, oblivious to her discomfort, he began carrying her two large suitcases up the stairs. 'I used to live there. I liked it, but if you don't, we can maybe come up with somewhere else.'

'No. No. It's fine.' She scurried after him, trying not to think that she was sleeping in her boss's bed.

'Good. Well, here we go.' He pushed open the door to her living quarters and strode in for all the world as if he owned the place. Which, Katie thought, he did, in a way.

The doctor carried her things through to the bedroom and unceremoniously dropped them on the bed. He returned, running his hands through his dark wavy hair.

'Were you all right last night? I asked Trish at the pub to look after you.'

'I didn't meet her,' Katie said. 'Scott brought some food over though, which

I think she had cooked.'

'Scott?' Adam frowned. 'Oh yes. Ed Collins's son. I just met him.'

His words caused Katie to do a double take. Ed? Wasn't that the name of the old man at the garage? But that meant Scott . . .

'Adam, give the poor girl some space.'

Before Katie could sort out the thoughts spinning in her head, a beautiful woman with short dark hair joined them.

'Hi. I'm Jess Gilmore. I fly the air ambulance and have the utter misfortune to be married to this crazy man here.'

The look the two shared put a lie to the latter part of that statement.

'Nice to meet you Jess.'

'I'm just going to drag Adam out of here, to give you a chance to settle in a bit,' Jess said. 'When you are ready, drop in to the office. I'll show you around and we can get the paperwork done.'

Jess ushered Adam out and began to pull the door closed behind her, then paused. 'Adam,' she called, 'we need to get Jack around to put a lock on this door.' She raised a hand and disappeared.

Katie stood in the middle of the room, still holding her bag of recent purchases, wondering if Coorah Creek was always like this. People coming and going, without due regard for . . . well for anything really. It appeared the people here were as foreign as her surroundings. And there were obviously things she had yet to find out; relationships and where Scott fitted in to the picture.

She shook her head. She'd feel better after a bath — or rather, a shower. There was no bath in her tiny bathroom. She took a couple of steps towards the bedroom and paused. Turning, she placed a chair under the knob of her door. She had no idea who this Jack was. If he was going to put a lock on her door, that was all to the good, but she didn't want him wandering in to do it while she was in the shower.

About an hour later, feeling much refreshed with clean skirt and shirt and teeth, she set out in search of the hospital office. It wasn't that hard to find. The hospital wasn't very big, and she could hear voices.

'Katie, come in,' Jess said when she spotted her loitering outside the office door. 'We were just chatting. Ken Travers, this is our new nurse, Katie.'

The middle-aged man was tall and thin, with receding hair and the slightly haunted air that Katie instantly recognised. This was a patient.

'Hello,' she said.

'Ken and I are just setting up his next appointment,' Jess said. 'He'll no doubt be pleased to have a real nurse here again, instead of putting up with my inexpert help.'

'Jess, you've been great,' the patient said with a smile. 'And welcome Katie. We are very glad to have you.'

With that he left.

Jess closed the appointment book as she watched him leave. Then she turned her attention to Katie. 'It is so good to have you here. I help Adam when I can — but I'm a pilot and he needs a real nurse.'

Katie remembered the young mother's words the night before. Jess had helped deliver her baby. They certainly did need a real nurse.

'What happened to your last nurse?'

To Katie's discomfort, a shadow of grief fell over Jess's face. Her eyes dimmed for a minute and she appeared lost in memory. Then she spoke in a voice that was infinitely sad. 'Sister Luke was our nurse for a long time. She was a medical nun. She and Adam were very close and when she died, Adam refused to look for a new nurse for a long time. Then he hired a couple, but they didn't work out. It takes a special kind of person to work all the way out here. But,' Jess took a deep breath and the sadness left her face, 'I'm sure you'll be great. Adam was up all night with a patient, and he's sleeping now, but I'll show you around.'

The hospital was small, but very well equipped. Jess explained that the money came from the Goongalla Uranium Mine — the town's main employer. There was a small and immaculate theatre where minor surgery was performed. Anything major and the patient was flown to the nearest big hospital at Mt Isa. The half-unpacked box of Christmas decorations sitting in the reception area was testament to the fact that the patients' needs came first. At least, that's how Katie chose to interpret it.

'You'll encounter all sorts of things here,' Jess warned. 'I could hardly believe it myself when I first arrived. You'll have to be ready to turn your hand to almost anything. We can't just call for extra help if the going gets tough. There is no one else, just this community.'

'Do you like it here?'

'I love it,' Jess said warmly. 'It's a unique place . . . full of interesting people. In fact, why don't you come and meet some of them this evening? We can grab a counter meal at the pub and introduce you around.'

'Okay.' Katie wasn't sure exactly what a 'counter meal' was, but she knew about eating in pubs. She had often eaten at the centuries old London pub near her home. She imagined Coorah Creek's pub would be very different, but she was willing to give it a go.

'But first things first,' Jess added. 'I need to get you introduced to the paperwork.'

9

Scott sat alone at one end of the long polished wood bar, staring morosely at the glistening tinsel on the Christmas tree. The cheerful decorations seemed almost to mock him as he lost himself in memories of Christmases past. He should have happy Christmas memories, but any he did have were overshadowed by the darkness of those later years when he and his father had lived alone, barely speaking to each other. Times when the holidays had been barely acknowledged in the house behind the garage. Dark times.

There was movement in the corner of his vision as his father walked into the pub.

A flash of surprise crossed Trish Warren's face as she looked up from pouring a beer and saw who her new customer was. Scott guessed his father didn't make a habit of going to the pub. Ed had never been the sociable type. Scott turned his attention back to the cold beer in front of him, running a finger through the wet droplets of condensation running down the glass onto the beer mat beneath.

'I guess I could join you for a drink.'

'I guess you could.'

Ed parked himself on the next bar stool. Not too close, but close enough for a conversation that would be as private as any conversation could be with Trish in the same room.

Scott took a pull on his beer, and watched out of hooded eyes as his father did the same with the glass of Fosters that Trish placed in front of him.

A palpable silence settled over them.

Where did you start, Scott wondered. After so many years, where did you start trying to reconnect? There wasn't going to be an apology on either side. Eight years was far too long for that. But there had to be some way to start rebuilding some sort of relationship. Ed was the only family he had and this was the only chance they were going to get to put the past behind them. But what could he say that wouldn't seem banal, or critical or at the very least draw attention to the huge gap between them?

'So. You're staying at the pub.'

It wasn't a question.

'Yes. I . . . ' Scott let his voice trail off. He didn't want to say that he thought he might not be welcome in his father's home. He also didn't want to say that he wasn't sure if he ever wanted to set foot inside that house again. Neither comment was going to help the two of them cross the enormous gulf that lay between them.

Silence settled again.

'That your Prius outside?'

'Yes.'

'Hybrid?'

'Yes.'

'Any good?'

'Yes.'

Maybe it was genetic. This thing about cars. In those dark years after his mother left, the only real conversations he and his father had shared had been about cars. The arguments had been about everything else. So Scott guessed it wasn't really surprising that this, the closest thing to a conversation they'd had in so many years, would be about a car.

The silence was back.

Scott was very conscious that his father was making some sort of effort. He was the one who had sought Scott out. And if his conversation has been stilted, at least he'd said more than just one word. But what could he say that wouldn't bring back the past?

The bar door swung open and some people walked in. Even before he looked up, Scott knew that Katie was one of them. He heard her laugh. She was with the doctor and an attractive dark-haired woman. As the three of them greeted Trish and found seats at the bar, the dark-haired woman and the doctor seemed to be always touching each other. A casual brush of fingers together, a hand on an arm. That spoke volumes, and Scott found he was secretly a little relieved. He didn't like the idea of Katie being around that doctor too much, but if he was already spoken for —

She saw him and her face lit up. His heart did a little skip when that happened. It dropped into a different rhythm as he watched her excuse herself from the doctor and start towards him. He was very conscious of his father's eyes moving from Scott, to Katie, and back again.

'Hi Scott!' She sounded pleased to see him.

'Hi Katie. Are you starting to feel a little more settled?'

She nodded, her blonde fringe bouncing in a most beguiling way. 'I wanted to say thanks for last night. For the dinner; and for staying. It really did help.'

'You're welcome,' Scott said, wondering what the rest of the people in the room would make of that exchange. They were so obviously all listening. This was the Coorah Creek he remembered, where everybody knew everybody else's business, especially if it involved who was sleeping with whom.

Katie hesitated for a moment. She looked from Scott to Ed and back again. Scott could see the question in her eyes. He wanted to say something, but he wasn't ready for that just yet.

A few moments passed in tense silence before Katie spoke again.

'Anyway, I'd like to return the favour sometime soon. Cook you dinner. If you'd like to?'

Of course he would. Those lovely blue eyes peeping out from under that fringe would entice any man. 'That sounds great,' he said.

Katie looked extremely pleased. A touch of colour lit her cheeks. 'Well, I guess I had better get back. I'm having dinner with the boss.'

'You'll be fine,' Scott said reassuringly. 'I only met him today for a few minutes, but he seems like a good bloke.' An even better bloke if he was safely married.

Katie nodded. As she turned to go, she spoke to Ed for the first time.

'I'm sorry. I hope I didn't interrupt anything.'

'No.'

She hesitated. 'I hope my car's — '

'It'll be ready Wednesday afternoon,' Ed said with a brusqueness that was all too familiar to Scott.

'All right.' Katie sounded very uncertain. She looked quickly from Scott to Ed and then back again, before smiling at both and turning away to re-join Doctor Adam.

'Ashamed of me, are you?' Ed said as she walked away. 'Didn't want to acknowledge me in front of the girl?'

Scott wanted to say yes, he was ashamed. He didn't want Katie to know he was the son of a man who cheated on his wife and hit his son. He didn't want her to know the blood that ran in his veins. But he'd come back to

Coorah Creek to make some sort of rapprochement, so he remained silent.

'I see. Well, you've got no grounds for moral superiority. Not if you spent the night with that girl when you barely knew her name.'

'It wasn't like that.' Scott got to his feet. He wasn't defending himself. After all these years, he didn't expect his father to have a very high opinion of him. And he didn't care either way. But he didn't want Katie's reputation damaged before she'd had a chance to establish herself in her new home. 'I was just helping someone who needed a friend. It's called kindness, but I don't expect you would know much about that.'

He walked away.

Leaving the pub by the back residents' entrance allowed Scott to avoid everyone — his father, Katie, Trish. All of them. Because right now he was in no fit state to talk to anyone. It was partly anger at his father. And partly anger at himself.

He cut through the back yard of the pub and leaped the low fence. Years ago, the land around the pub had all been empty. Now there were houses facing the road, but he was still able to skirt the back fences. That left him facing another low fence. He leaned on it and looked over into the school grounds. The school was a lot bigger now than in his day. There were new blocks of classrooms, a small swimming pool and what looked like a big hall. So much had changed. But not him.

That's why he was angry with himself. He'd come all this way seeking to heal the rift with his father. If not heal it, at least build some sort of bridge over it. While he still could. Because in a few weeks, he'd be travelling to the other side of the world. And he might never come back.

He wasn't an angry teenager any more. He was a grown man who should be able to put old hurts aside and at least have a civil conversation with his father. But every time he looked at the old man, he felt that angry boy rise back to the surface.

He closed his eyes, picturing the town as it had been. The school ground as it had been. He tried to remember the last time his mother had come to watch him play cricket on the dry cracked pitch just in front of where he was now standing.

His mother had been beautiful. He still remembered the pretty white dress she'd worn on that last hot day. He still remembered the long brown hair that she pulled back into a ponytail. He still remembered; but he didn't. The hardest thing he had to do, even harder than talk to his father, was admit to himself that he no longer remembered his mother's face. Or the sound of her voice.

And for that, he would never forgive his father.

10

Something was banging. Hard. Loud. Katie tentatively opened her eyes. It was still dark. She closed her eyes again and groaned. The banging didn't go away. She had barely had anything to drink last night. And she'd come to bed early as the jet lag cut in. So this wasn't a hangover.

Why then was there banging?

She opened her eyes again, and this time acknowledged that a very faint light might just be visible at the edge of the bedroom curtains. Slowly she got out of bed and rubbing her eyes, walked through to the lounge room of her new living quarters.

The banging was even louder here.

'All right. I'm coming!'

She opened the door, blinking against the light that poured in from the well-lit hallway. By the third blink, she registered Adam standing in front of her. She pushed her hair out of her eyes as, at the same moment, she registered that she was in her pyjamas. Oh dear.

'We've got to get to the airport,' Adam said briskly, taking no notice of her attire. 'There's been an accident. We have to fly to Galbarra Station right away.'

'Ah ... Okay.' The urgency in Adam's voice helped Katie to gather her scattered wits.

'Jess is already on her way to the airstrip. I'm just going to collect some supplies. Get ready as fast as you can and we'll take my car.'

'All right.'

It didn't take long. Katie threw some water over her face and cleaned her teeth. She hesitated for a moment at the half unpacked suitcase sitting on the bedroom floor. Back in England, the hospital had a uniform code she'd had to abide by. Plain cotton scrubs that were as practical as they were hideous. If there was such a uniform code in Coorah

Creek, she had yet to learn it. She hesitated for no more than a moment, remembering the urgency in Adam's voice. Then she threw on a clean denim skirt and a blue top. She didn't bother grabbing a jacket. In this scorching part of the world, she didn't need one. A few moments later she was walking smartly through to the hospital, where Adam was waiting.

Katie had done her fair share of flying. Even before her global journey, there had been trips to Ibiza and Greece. The cut price holiday flights had taken her to some pretty basic airports. But nothing like the one at Coorah Creek. It wasn't an airport. It was a tin shed. The plane that was waiting for them was so small it looked almost like a toy in the dim light of the dawn. It was sitting on what looked more like a short bit of road than any sort of runway. The nearest of the tall gum trees looked far too close for comfort. And she expected a kangaroo to hop past at any moment. Definitely not Katie's idea of an airport.

Adam parked his car next to the shed. As Katie got out, Jess appeared from the depths of the shed, carrying a rucksack.

'I made us coffee,' she said as she led the way to the plane.

The inside of the tiny aircraft was a revelation. There were stretchers bolted to the walls, with belts no doubt to hold the patients in. Well-designed lockers everywhere would no doubt hold a wealth of medical equipment. It reminded Katie of an ambulance which, she guessed, was exactly what it was. An ambulance with wings.

'Why don't you sit up front this time?' Adam asked as he pulled up the narrow stairs and fastened the door.

'Up front?'

'The co-pilot's seat. I usually sit there. You get a great view.'

'I don't want to take . . . '

'It's fine,' Jess was already buckling herself into the pilot's seat. 'It'll be nice to have someone new to keep me company. Adam usually falls asleep as soon as we're in the air.'

With a derisive snort, the doctor lowered himself into one of the very comfortable looking seats. Katie hesitantly moved towards the front of the plane. She heard a low whine followed by a coughing splutter as the propellers began to slowly move. Then the engine roared into life. She slid into her seat, fumbling with the unfamiliar seatbelt.

'Let me help.' Jess leaned over and efficiently snapped the seatbelt into place.

The whole plane was vibrating as Jess increased the power and turned the pointy nose towards the runway. With one hand she reached for a microphone. With a shock Katie realised Jess was alerting any nearby aircraft to her imminent take-off. Didn't they have air traffic control out here?

Katie's thoughts were interrupted by the roar of the twin engines as Jess sent the small plane hurtling down the tarmac stip. Katie grabbed the arms of her seat, her fingernails digging in to the surface as the plane shook and bounced. The trees along the fence line were approaching at terrifying speed, and still they had not left the ground. The end of the runway flashed beneath them, as at the last possible moment, the plane lifted into the air and began to climb into the early morning sky. A few seconds later, when the ground still seemed scarily close, Jess banked the plane heavily. The engine roar was incredibly loud as they continued to climb. Katie glanced down and saw the red earth dropping away. The town was growing rapidly smaller, the buildings shrinking until they seemed like toys.

Katie felt her stomach roil. No. No. She wasn't going to throw up. She shut her eyes, but that only made it worse. Taking a deep breath, she tried to focus her eyes on something inside the aircraft, rather than dropping away below her. She watched Jess's hands on the controls. She seemed to know what she was doing. That should be a comfort.

Suddenly, the world dropped away. Katie felt herself falling for several seconds before the seat rose to kick her in the behind. Terrified, she glanced at Jess, but the pilot seemed unconcerned. Jess played with the array of instruments and dials in front of her, as once more the tiny aircraft lurched.

'Sorry about that,' Jess said turning her way at last. 'It's often a bit bumpy first thing in the morning. We've reached our cruising height now. It's only a short trip. Less than an hour. But that should give you time to enjoy the scenery.'

Enjoy the scenery? She had to be joking.

Katie's fingers remained tightly clenched on the arms of the seat as she took long slow breaths to calm herself. When the frantic beating of her heart had slowed to something approaching normal, she risked a glance out of the window. The world spun and she closed her eyes again against the image of a wide flat brown plain, with not a single sign of human habitation. Where on earth were they?

An overwhelming sense of strangeness and of isolation swept through her. Beside her, Jess was chatting away, seeming not to notice that Katie was frozen with fear.

The plane's nose suddenly dipped, and Katie had to bite back a cry of terror.

'There it is,' Jess indicated with a nod as she reached for the radio handset.

There *what* was? Katie risked another quick glance out of the window. She could see nothing except the never-ending plain. Jess was talking to someone on the radio as the aircraft began a steep and swift descent that had Katie's stomach churning violently. Still clutching the armrest as if her life might depend upon it, Katie stared straight ahead into the wide blue sky. But as the plane banked again, she caught a glimpse of a small cluster of buildings in front and below them. But there was nothing to suggest an airport?

Lower and lower the plane dropped. Katie was trying desperately not to throw up as her stomach rebelled again even more strongly. Then she saw what they were heading for. No! It was just a line in the red earth. No tarmac. No buildings. No . . . nothing. Just bare dirt. Surely Jess wasn't planning to land there?

She was and she did.

The tiny aircraft touched down then rolled and bounced across the uneven dirt. It seemed to take forever to stop. Katie opened the eyes she had kept tightly shut during the landing and glanced over her shoulder. Adam was shaking his head as if he'd just been woken by the bumps. Beside her, Jess was doing her pilot thing. But all Katie cared about was getting solid earth under her feet again.

By the time Katie was out of her seat, Adam had the door open. He was passing a couple of medical bags to someone outside. That brought home to Katie just what they were doing there. She was a nurse and someone was hurt. Her knees were shaking as she carefully descended the narrow aircraft steps. There were two vehicles waiting, both old and battered and driven by men who looked pretty well-used themselves. Adam gestured to her to take the cab of the small pick-up truck, and then he leaped into the back.

The driver gunned his engine as the vehicle lurched forward. Katie looked about for a seatbelt then gave up. She tried to calm her mind. She had a job to do. She would forget all about the flight and concentrate on her patient. The vehicle hit a pot hole and Katie grabbed the dashboard as she was thrown about in her seat.

'Sorry,' the driver said. 'This track needs grading.'

Katie said nothing, her whole being focused on the job she had to do at the end of her journey — if she survived.

11

'I need a word with you, Ed.'

Ed jumped slightly, and banged his knuckles on the engine block. Rubbing his hand, he withdrew from under the car's bonnet and straightened. Trish Warren was standing in the doorway of the workshop.

'What can I do for you Trish?'

She came into the workshop. She looked around for somewhere to sit, but obviously rejected all the options. Ed had to admit the place was messy but it *was* a workshop.

'I came to say it's high time you joined in the Waifs and Orphans this year. We could use your help setting up. There's always so much work to do. With the party getting bigger every year, the workload just gets bigger too. And of course you are very welcome at the party.'

Ed sighed. The annual town Christmas party was Trish's special project. Every year she tried to get him involved and every year she failed. Not that she ever stopped trying. Trish was nothing if not determined.

'Now Trish,' he said. 'We've had this conversation before. You know that I don't care for Christmas.'

'Rubbish. Everybody loves Christmas. I remember years ago, your house used to be covered with lights. And you hosted a Christmas barbecue too. So don't tell me you don't care for Christmas.'

'Things changed.' Ed felt the first rumbling of annoyance. Trish knew as well as anyone what had destroyed his Christmas. Perhaps better than anyone, because he was sure her gossiping had only made matters so much worse.

'They did.' Trish's voice softened. 'But they are changing again Ed. Surely you see that. You don't want to miss this chance.'

She was right, of course. He didn't. But he wasn't entirely sure what to do.

A chance was a fragile thing. Easily broken and lost.

He absently picked up a rag to wipe his greasy hands.

'The party is going to be great this year,' Trish told him. 'It'll serve as a welcome for that new nurse, Katie. And I think Scott is going to stay for it. He's just extended the booking on his room at the hotel.'

Ed looked up sharply.

'How long is he staying?'

'At least a couple more weeks.'

'He's probably staying because of that nurse. She's very pretty and I think they may have something going on.' His voice betrayed his uncertainty.

'Oh, they definitely have something going on.' Trish was obviously pleased to impart that news. 'But does it really matter why he stays?'

She was right. He studied her face and saw the kindness in her eyes. She was a terrible gossip, but she was smarter than she looked. And she had a heart of gold. Trish and her pub were very much the heart of this community.

'All right.' Ed gave way as gracefully as he could. 'What do you need me to do?'

'There'll be working party over at the hall in a few days. They'll need all the help they can get. And you had better show up at the party too or I'll come and drag you down there myself.'

'All right.'

Trish nodded, obviously pleased with herself. She started to walk back to the pub, but stopped in the doorway. 'By the way, you might want to stroll over when you close up. The beef stew is particularly good tonight.'

Ed watched her retreating back and wondered what that was all about. It was almost closing time so he walked outside to lock the petrol bowsers. As he did, he looked across at the pub. Through the open windows he could see a lone figure sat at the bar. Ah. Now he understood. Trish was meddling again.

He went back inside, locking the workshop behind him. Candy met him as he crossed the yard towards the house. She looked at him and whined softly. He patted her.

Maybe Trish had a point. He turned around but changed his mind. It wouldn't hurt to clean up just a little before he went to the pub.

* * *

When should we expect to see you?

The words on Scott's laptop screen glowed in an almost accusing manner. The e-mail had arrived yesterday, but he still hadn't answered it.

We will take delivery of the two cars — the Lancia and the Mercedes in mid-January, and would be keen for you to begin work on them immediately to have at least one of them ready for exhibition in the summer.

They meant the English summer of course. To restore either of those cars would take a good six or seven months of hard work.

He looked at the signature and the

distinctive logo. As a teenage rev-head with a passion for classic cars, he'd dreamed about working for a place like that. He could still hardly believe that one of the world's great motor museums wanted him to restore and care for their beautiful machines. When he started his own small restoration workshop in Brisbane five years ago, he'd worked twenty hours a day to build his business. A chance meeting with the owner of that signature had resulted in this dream of a job offer.

He was going, of course. He'd be a fool to pass it up. He'd already sold his workshop. That money would help him establish himself in England and start the new life he'd always wanted. A life far, far away from Coorah Creek. After all, there was nothing to hold him here. No-one to hold him here. Not even many memories. At least, not good memories.

Still his fingers hesitated over the laptop keys.

This trip wasn't going quite the way he had planned.

A few weeks ago, while selling his business and preparing to move to the other side of the world, he had begun thinking about what to take to his new life. And what he was going to leave behind. His few mates had already invited themselves to visit him in England. He'd never really had a serious girlfriend. He was leaving nothing behind — because he had nothing to leave.

His mother was long gone. He didn't know where she was or even, to be brutally honest, if she was still alive. Sitting there in his workshop, packing up his tools, another thought had struck with the force of a cyclone. At that moment, he also hadn't known if his father was dead or alive. For the first time in almost a decade, he was overcome with a desire to go back to Coorah Creek. He had to see his father one more time before he shook the Aussie dust from his feet and headed for greener pastures.

He hadn't expected a rapprochement. There was too much bad blood to be healed. He has just . . . What?

Now that he was here, he was even less sure.

He hadn't expected to feel . . . anything.

Maybe finding Candy still alive had stirred up too many emotions. Made him vulnerable. Or maybe it was the realisation that his father was now a lonely old man. Whatever it was, he found he didn't hate his father as much as he'd thought. He wasn't ready to forgive him. But maybe he could let go of his anger.

He had some time. Christmas was a couple of weeks away and he'd already talked to Trish about keeping the hotel room until then. He didn't need to be in the UK until the second week in January. He could easily move his flight back to the New Year.

He stared out the window, and caught a flash of sunlight. The air ambulance was coming in for a landing. He wondered if Katie was on board. Probably. He wondered how she had managed on this first flight. Perhaps he could drop by her place this evening. After all, he felt a little responsible for her. He'd rescued her twice already. Maybe she'd need rescuing again. Or maybe she'd just want some company. That wouldn't be a bad thing. Nothing would ever come of it, of course. He didn't do relationships. Not really. Not only that, Katie had come to Coorah Creek to live. He had come to say goodbye. But until then, they could be friends, couldn't they.

There was absolutely no reason to think she had anything to do with his reluctance to send the e-mail that he knew he had to send.

Taking a deep breath, he began to type . . .

I expect to arrive in the UK shortly after New Year. I'll be in touch as soon as I arrive. I am very much looking forward to starting work on the cars.

He signed off and hit send.

It was probably too soon to go looking for Katie. While he waited, it wouldn't hurt to do a bit more research on that

Lancia. He'd never restored one of those before. He wanted to get it right.

Within minutes he was lost in his favourite place — a world of rare and beautiful classic cars. He was so engrossed in what he was doing, he didn't hear the heavy footsteps crossing the bar's polished wooden floor.

'Now that's a nice car.'

Ed pulled up a stool next to Scott.

'It sure is.'

'Ever since you were a kid, you wanted one of those. You had an old owner's manual. The '75 model. Always had your nose in it.'

Neither of them mentioned that the Lancia owner's manual was one of the things Scott had taken with him the day he turned his back on his father and the town of Coorah Creek. It was now sitting in a box in the boot of his car.

'I'm surprised you remember.' Scott had trouble keeping the bitterness out of his voice.

'I remember a lot more than you think.'

There seemed to be nothing he could say to that.

Scott closed that internet window, leaving another displayed. It was the home page for the National Museum of Motoring. The place he would soon be working.

'Now, there's a place I always wanted to visit,' Ed said slowly. 'All those wonderful European cars. I've never even seen a Rolls Royce out here — far less something like an old Aston Martin or a Lotus. I'd love to look under the bonnet of something like that. Just once in my life.'

Scott was startled by the emotion in his father's voice. A profound sadness. It had never occurred to him that the old man might have such strong regrets.

'Why didn't you go there? A holiday or something.'

'I didn't want to be gone from here . . . '

The words fell into the space between them. Surely his father wasn't still hoping his mother would come back? Or . . . had his father stayed here all those years hoping Scott would come back?

The silence was becoming a little hard to take. Scott finished closing down his computer. The click as he shut the lid seemed very loud.

'That car's done.' Once again, it was his father taking the lead.

'Car?'

'The girl's.'

'Oh. I thought you weren't going to have it ready until tomorrow.'

'The parts arrived this morning. It didn't take long then. I thought you might take it back to her.'

That was a surprise. Scott looked at his father and raised an eyebrow.

'Well,' Ed said. 'The two of you seemed . . . friendly.'

Scott wanted to laugh. After all this time, his father was matchmaking? Maybe he was hoping Scott might hang around if he was involved with Katie. It wasn't a bad prospect — but he had a job waiting.

'Don't you want her to pay for it before she picks it up?'

Ed shook his head slowly. 'Son, you sure have forgotten a lot about this town. This isn't the city. We do things differently. She needs the damn car. Take it to her. She can pay me next time she's passing.'

Scott took the keys his father held out, thinking as he did that his father was right. There were many, many things he had forgotten. And maybe not all of them were bad.

12

Katie's knees were shaking so much, she almost fell to the ground as she came down the steps of the aircraft. As her feet touched good solid earth, she heaved a sigh of relief, then heaved again as her stomach lurched. She covered her mouth with her hand, and stepped away from the plane. Just in case. When she had her stomach under control, she turned to see Adam coming out of the plane, a brown bag in his hands. Her humiliation was complete as her boss carried the air sick bag over to the tin shed and deposited it in a big metal drum of rubbish.

'Don't feel too bad.' Jess joined Katie on the tarmac and placed a comforting hand on her shoulder. 'Everybody does that at least once in their lives.'

'Did you?' Katie asked.

'Well, no. But I'm a pilot. We're not

allowed to get air sick.'

And she was a nurse. She wasn't supposed to get air sick either. Thank goodness there hadn't been a patient on board. The injured stockman had been treated and left at the station in his wife's care.

'Don't worry about it,' Adam offered as he joined them again. 'We'll leave Jess to take care of the plane, and I can take you home. You'll feel better when you freshen up and have a nice cup of tea.'

The mere thought of putting anything into her stomach almost made her ill again. But the doctor was right. By the time she had returned to her flat, had a shower and donned some fresh clothes, she was feeling better. She boiled the kettle and made some mint tea. Someone had once told her mint tea was good for an upset stomach. It was, but not good enough to give her back her energy, or take away the ache in her back.

She lay back on her sofa and closed her eyes.

She tried to empty her mind, but she couldn't. Her mind was churning as badly as her stomach had earlier in the day. One thought was pounding into her brain over and over again.

She had made a terrible mistake coming to Coorah Creek. She felt tears welling up in her eyes, and squeezed her lids even more tightly to stop them overflowing down her cheeks. She had only been here a few days, but already she hated Coorah Creek! Hated it!

She hated the heat. And the isolation. At night, the silence was so overwhelming it kept her awake. She hated the fact that there were no coffee shops or shops of any sort. And she hated working somewhere without structure or uniforms or rules or all the things that made up a proper hospital.

But most of all she hated flying in the air ambulance!

Her stomach twisted again at the mere thought.

It wasn't that she was afraid of flying. She was quite happy in a big jet with hundreds of other passengers. But that little plane . . . She could open a window and put her hand out — into nothingness. The plane was totally vulnerable to the wind and the clouds. The mere thought of running into a storm made her shudder. She never NEVER wanted to go up in that plane again.

But she had to. It was part of her job, and she loved her job. At least, she had loved her job. Once. She loved being able to help people — watching someone regain their health and strength. But working in a large hospital had taken that away from her. She had hated the overwhelming workload that left her exhausted. Hated being too busy to really connect with any one patient. It was so impersonal. And there was also the mad scramble for advancement. The politics of the place had involved a much greater degree of back stabbing and bitchiness than she had ever expected.

And there were the doctors. She

shuddered as she remembered a couple of confrontations. One in particular. A senior consultant. She's seen him miss something and had tried to bring it to his attention. She'd been tactful and done it by asking a question. He'd simply dismissed her. Only when she'd been insistent had he realised his mistake. Katie had saved the patient some unnecessary discomfort, but that doctor had never forgiven her for finding his flaw. Nor had the doctor whose advances she had refused. They weren't all like that, of course. There were good doctors as well as bad. It just seemed to her, in the pressure cooker of a large hospital, the bad seemed to surface more often.

Katie had no illusions. She understood the need for rules and regulations and order in a big hospital. She didn't mind the hard work and she could even cope with the doctors who stepped over the line. But that wasn't the sort of nursing she wanted to do. That's why she'd left and come here. As far from that London medical machine as she could get. Here she had hoped to find a more personal approach to medicine. And she was right. This was more personal, more rewarding. Except for the flying. That was a nightmare. She hated herself for the fear that had left her either paralysed — or being violently sick. But hating herself was not going to make it any better.

And now look at her, lying on a couch wallowing in self-pity! What sort of behaviour was that? It was time she pulled herself together.

She opened her eyes, brushed away the moisture and stared up at the ceiling. Above her, the big fan was going round and round, in long slow sweeps. And round. And . . .

Katie sat up quickly, her hand on her stomach. She stood quickly and made a bee-line for the bathroom. She opened the door and her eyes fell upon a monstrous spider, all black and hairy, poised on the edge of the toilet seat. It seemed to be watching her. Its beady eyes glinted as it raised its front legs in a menacing fashion.

Katie screamed.

Almost instantly there was a pounding on her door.

'Katie! Katie! Are you all right?'

She spun away from the bathroom and its fearsome denizen and flung herself across the room to her door. She struggled for a few seconds with her newly installed lock, before reefing the door open and literally falling into Scott's open arms.

'Hey. What's wrong? Are you all right?'

She nodded wordlessly into the front of his shirt.

'Come on. Sit down and tell me what's going on.'

She shook her head, digging her toes in and refusing to be led back to the flat. She struggled to get control of her breathing and finally pulled herself together enough to speak.

'That giant spider from Lord of The Rings is in my bathroom.'

'Oh. Well, I guess I had better deal with it, then.'

'Please!' To her own ears she sounded pathetic.

Totally unconcerned, not to mention unarmed, Scott headed for her bathroom. He vanished through the doorway. She heard some scuffling noises, and then what sounded like the window being opened and closed.

'There you are,' Scott emerged smiling. 'Just like Frodo. I did the hero thing.'

'Frodo didn't fight Shelob. Sam did.' Katie automatically corrected him. 'And he didn't kill her.'

'That's all right. I didn't kill this one either. I just put it outside.'

'But it might come back!'

'It's just a huntsman. Totally harmless you know.'

'It didn't look harmless.' Katie's breathing was starting to return to normal. 'Sorry I overreacted. I've had a rough day.'

'Sorry to hear it. Well, I have good

news for you. Your car is fixed. I brought it round for you in case you needed it.'

So — you've rescued me again. This is becoming a habit.'

'Always glad to help.'

He smiled and Katie's heart did a little flip that had nothing to do with the spider.

'I'll tell you what,' Scott said, 'if you're up to it, there's a place I'd like to show you. It's one of my favourite places. It might help cheer you up.'

Katie looked into his handsome and eager face. She had no idea where he was taking her, but one thing she did know. Spending a bit of time with Scott would certainly put a little bit of joy back in her day.

'Okay,' she said.

'Great.' He handed over the keys to her car. 'You can drive this time.'

13

The track to the creek looked just the same to Scott. It was just two tyre ruts in the rough ground. It may have become a little deeper over the years, but nothing else had changed.

'Are you sure?' Katie had pulled up just off the main road, and was staring down the dusty track, her brow wrinkled in a frown.

'You'll be fine,' he assured her. 'Good Aussie cars are built for roads like this. Just keep your wheels in the tracks and take it easy.'

Katie's response was a dubious sigh, but she put the car in gear and edged forward. 'If I do any damage, it'll be on you,' she said.

Despite her misgivings, Katie handled the rough going well. The car travelled smoothly, if slowly, down the track towards the line of gum trees that marked the creek bank. Scott suppressed a smile as he watched the concentration on her face and the careful way her hands gripped the steering wheel. Katie might be out of her depth here in the outback, but she wasn't about to let it beat her. She had strengths and abilities that maybe she hadn't even found yet. He liked that about her.

He liked watching her. He liked the way she bit her lower lip as she concentrated. He liked the way she could laugh at herself and he really liked the way her blue eyes sparkled when she did.

Finally, they reached the creek. Katie didn't need his guidance as she instinctively parked the car under the trees, out of the hot sun. The bare dirt and a few bits of litter indicated this place was more frequently used now than when young Scott Collins used to come here. Before he was old enough to drive, he'd ridden a pushbike. Once or twice he'd used his father's car, hoping not to be caught. Now the town had grown, he imagined many more kids would be seeking this place out.

As Scott opened the door and got out of the car, he saw movement in the long dry grass as a snake slithered away. It was just a carpet snake. Harmless. But he decided not to mention it to Katie. She'd seen enough of the local wildlife already today.

They moved to the front of the car and looked down the sloping bank to the creek.

'There's not a lot of water.' Katie sounded disappointed.

'Not at this time of the year,' Scott said. He took a couple of steps down the bank then turned to offer her a hand down. It wasn't that he thought she needed his help. In fact, he was sure she didn't. He just wanted an excuse to hold her hand.

Katie started to shake her head, then her eyes met and held his. Understanding passed between them and she placed her hand in his. It felt good to curl his fingers around her small hand

and offer her whatever strength he had.

They made their way down the slope. She sat down on an old tree trunk that had washed down the river in some flood many years before. It was hard and bleached to a pale grey by the sun, but was a convenient place to sit overlooking the slow-moving shallow waterway that was Coorah Creek.

He sat next to her. Close enough that he could hear her breathing.

'I had imagined a deep river, with a tyre on a rope that local teenagers use as a swing to jump out into the water,' Katie said.

'There's never enough water for that,' Scott said. 'And when I was growing up here, there weren't that many teenagers either.'

'But the school looks quite large,' Katie said.

'It's grown since the mine came. Back then, there was one building and one teacher. The teacher dealt with the little kids. In a separate room, the older kids did School of The Air.'

'What's that?'

'We did our lessons via radio with a teacher somewhere else.'

'That's very cool!'

'I suppose so. There were only five or six of us. Not enough to justify another teacher. And we were the kids whose parents were too poor to send us off to boarding school. I guess some places still do it now . . . although I imagine the internet has changed things a bit.'

'I guess a lot has changed since then.'

Yes, Scott thought. A lot has changed. But a lot has stayed exactly the same. He cast a sideways glance at Katie. She was swinging her feet above the ground. She looked so young. And sweet. For an instant he could imagine she was one of the teenagers who so obviously came here now. He could imagine that he was younger too. The boy he'd been before circumstances, and his father's fists, made him grow up so very very fast.

They sat in silence for a while. Scott had expected Katie to ask about his past. But she didn't. She seemed content with the person he was now. And to let him tell her what he wanted at his own speed. Somehow that made him more willing to tell her.

'You know Ed? Who fixed your car. He's my father.'

'I know.' Katie turned to look at him, her blue eyes shadowed. 'Adam told me.'

'I should have realised. Nothing stays private for long in this town.'

'I did wonder why you didn't say anything. Particularly when we were in the pub together.'

'It's a long story. And not a good one.'

Katie frowned. 'Something happened between you?'

'Yeah . . . Before this week, I hadn't seen or spoken to him since my seventeenth birthday.'

'That's a long time.'

He knew that. That day seemed an eternity ago. It seemed like yesterday.

'My mum was gone.' The words came of their own volition. 'She left when I

138

was about twelve. I didn't understand it. I loved her so much and I just couldn't believe that she would go away without me. My father has never really been a cheerful or demonstrative person. After she left, he become positively sullen and withdrawn. He put away everything in the house that reminded him of her. He wouldn't talk about her, even though I really needed to. I managed to keep just one photo. I guess that was the advantage of those old photo prints. I hid one where he couldn't find it. I used to look at it and wonder where she was. I vowed that one day, when I was old enough, I would go and find her.'

'Did your father ever tell you why she left?'

'For a very long time I thought it was me. I thought I'd done something wrong to chase her away.'

'No!' The exclamation wasn't loud — but it was passionate. Katie's hand reached out to cover his. 'It wasn't that. I am sure of it.'

His fingers and hers intertwined and

he held her tightly.

'I know that now. Just a few days after my seventeenth birthday, I was at the shop, buying some food for my dog, Candy. I thought Candy was the only one who loved me. I heard someone talking. About my father. He'd had an affair. That was why my mother left.'

'Oh, Scott.' The compassion in her voice seemed to envelope him and warm him, even as the flood of words continued.

'I went back to the house. I was just a kid and I was so angry. I demanded to know why he did it. As I confronted him I realised for the first time that I was as big as he was. I yelled at him. I blamed him for everything. He just stood there and said nothing. Then I hit him.'

'What did he do?'

'He hit me back. Knocked me down. I got right back up and hit him again.'

'And . . . '

'He knocked me down again. There was something on his face. A blankness.

When I got back up the second time, I just walked away. I grabbed a few things and walked out that door.'

'Where did you go?'

'I went across the road to the pub. My head was spinning and my hand hurt like hell. My knuckles were bleeding. I tried to buy a beer. I figured I was a man now and could handle it. When Trish Warren wouldn't serve me, I put my fist through her window. Guess that shows how much of a man I really wasn't. And it left my hand hurting even more.'

She smiled. It was a slow sad smile, but to Scott it felt as warm as the sun.

'And . . . '

'I left Coorah Creek that night. Hitched a ride on a passing truck. I was determined to find my mother. I haven't been back since — until you and I drove into town together.'

'And you never found her?'

'No. I eventually got a job and started working. With cars. That's irony for you. Then I went to night school to finish my education.'

'And now you're back.'

Scott hesitated. He didn't want to say that he was leaving. Going to England. That seemed some sort of betrayal of this moment. Of this strange intimacy that had suddenly come to pass with Katie. He closed his hand even more tightly around hers. 'I just felt it was time to see if — Well, maybe we could make amends.'

'And are you?'

That was a very good question. 'We haven't hit each other,' he said with a wry grin. 'I guess that's something.'

'It's a start.'

'Yeah. There's a lot to make up for. The years between Mum leaving and me leaving were not good. Dad was in a bad place. I can see that now. He took me there too. There was no joy in the house. And none for me anywhere else either. Dad made sure I was fed and clothed, but that was it.'

'That must have been horrible. But a lot of time has passed. You have to at least try to mend the bridges. If you don't, and you lose him too, you will come to regret it.'

He sighed. 'How did you get to be so wise?'

'I come from a pretty close family. I know how much they mean to me. I couldn't imagine how hard it must have been without that.'

'I missed out on a lot of the fun of being a teenager. The other kids always ostracised me because I was Ed Collins's son. When they came here for parties, I was never invited. They came here to make out with their girlfriends, but I always came alone. I should have had my first kiss here with pretty little Alice Lake from school. It never happened.'

A gentle silence seemed to settle around them. The breeze in the trees faded. The ripples on the water seemed to sigh into stillness. The world around them held its breath as the silence grew.

'It could happen now.' Katie's voice was soft and inviting.

Scott didn't need to be told twice. Feeling not unlike a nervous teenager, he leaned forward and his lips touched Katie's. Gently. Softly. With great tenderness. There was an innocence to the kiss that seemed to wash away all the ugliness of his memories. His heart jumped and in that heartbeat, some of his lost youth returned to him. After a few seconds, they moved apart, just enough to breathe. Scott looked down into Katie's lovely face. This was not Alice — the girl of his teenage fantasies. The girl who shunned him. This was Katie. A warm and beautiful woman, whose shining eyes were all the invitation he needed.

When he kissed her the second time, it was as a man kisses a woman.

14

Maybe Coorah Creek wasn't really such a bad place. Katie pulled some dressings from the storage cupboard and headed back towards the treatment room. The past few days had been good days. With both feet firmly planted on solid ground, she'd been working at the hospital with Adam.

It still seemed strange to be calling the doctor by his first name. That wasn't how they did things back home. There were a lot of things about this hospital and this job that weren't like they were back home. She wasn't wearing a uniform. There were no rules and regulations. Patients came in without appointments. And they brought things. The young couple she'd met on her first day here had brought flowers with them this morning when they brought their daughter for a check-up. An aboriginal man from one of the outlying cattle properties had come by — not for treatment, but to drop off a painting for Adam as a belated wedding gift. The painting was beautiful. It was just a brown canvas covered with brown dots, but somehow it seemed to evoke a wonderful sense of this place that was literally out the back of nowhere.

Everything was a bit strange.

But she had to admit Adam was a very good doctor. She enjoyed working with him. His focus on his patients was total, and she enjoyed being there to assist. To hand him the things he needed before he asked for them. That was what she had trained for. She had started taking over the office paperwork from Jess too. There was a lot to learn. Australia's health system was very different to the British one. But she'd figure it out.

And then there was Scott.

Since that first kiss down by the creek, they had seen each other every day. They had met twice in the pub for dinner. And there had been another trip to the creek bank. This time with some beer and a picnic basket. But tonight, Scott was coming to her place for dinner. And she was as eager as a teenager on her first date.

Which was ridiculous when you thought that Scott had spent the night on her couch the day they met. They hadn't spent the night together since. That kiss down by the creek had changed everything. But tonight, maybe . . .

'Katie?'

Adam's voice dragged her back to reality. She was standing in the open doorway of the treatment room, her arms full of the dressings that Adam needed for the injured mine worker whose arm was currently swathed in slightly bloody cloth.

'Sorry.' She darted forward to do her job, all thoughts of Scott pushed hurriedly to the back of her mind.

He didn't stay there though. As soon as she was no longer needed at the hospital, Katie drove to the town's store to get what she needed. She had already discovered that the store's supplies were generous in number but not very broad in content. Obviously artichoke hearts and anchovies were not popular items on home menus in Coorah Creek. Still, she wasn't a bad cook and was sure she'd come up with something.

Behind the serving counter, Ken Travers raised a hand in greeting as she entered the store. He'd been back for another appointment just yesterday. She'd seen the test results and they weren't good. That, she knew, was the disadvantage of this more personal style of nursing. It was harder to accept the bad news when your patient was more than just a number and a chart.

The store was looking festive with tinsel along the shelves, shiny globes glinting in the afternoon sunlight and cotton wool pretending to be snow along the window ledge. Katie had almost forgotten about Christmas. Back home, the shops in Oxford Street started getting all dressed for the season in October. But here it was, just a couple of weeks to go, and the store had only just placed a huge box of Christmas decorations by the front counter to attract shoppers. She walked over and picked up some shiny gold tinsel. Christmas. That didn't seem right when she was standing there in a tank top and shorts. It wasn't supposed to be 100 degrees at Christmas. And there was no point in crossing her fingers and hoping for snow. A white Christmas was never going to happen out here.

A wave of homesickness hit her so hard, she felt tears prick the back of her eyes. She had wanted this adventure. This chance to rethink her life and her career choices . . . but now that she was alone, she missed them all terribly. E-mail and Facebook helped, but Katie knew in her heart that this Christmas would not bring her the joy she always felt at home, around the fireplace with her family.

She allowed herself only a moment of self-pity then shook it off. This Christmas was going to be exciting. A new place. New friends. Scott . . .

Would he be spending Christmas with his father? And then what? He hadn't talked about leaving, but she remembered his words on the day they met. Just visiting for a while. That's what he'd said. He'd come back to try to mend his relationship with his father. But then what? Would he just drive away and not look back?

She didn't want to examine that thought too closely. Instead, she began to rummage around in the box of decorations. There was some tinsel that wasn't too tatty. Some nice shiny glass baubles. Even a star for the top of the tree she didn't have. Surely she could get one though? She didn't think for one minute she could buy one — but someone around here must own an axe. There were plenty of trees about. It might be fun to have a gum tree instead of a pine tree in her flat.

As for snow — well, there was plenty of cotton wool at the hospital. She'd make do.

She assembled her decorations, and started collecting the ingredients for the evening's dinner. Scott was bringing the wine. Maybe he could help her acquire a tree of some sort and they could decorate it together. Her spirits lifted even more. That would be fun! She vaguely heard a telephone ringing, but was too caught up with her plans to pay any attention, until Ken called her to his counter.

'That was Adam on the phone,' he told her in a low urgent voice. 'He needs you at the airstrip right now.'

'Now?' her heart sank.

'Yep. Leave that stuff. I'll get it over to the hospital for you later. Adam sounded like it was urgent.'

Katie wanted to swear. Having no mobile phone service should have made her harder to find. But not when everyone in town knew everybody else in town and where they were at any given moment. Still . . . whoever needed medical care would be grateful she was that easy to find.

She left the store and drove straight to the airport. Jess already had the plane on the runway. Adam reached down through the open door and helped her on board. The plane was taxiing before she was even strapped in. Katie clenched her hands around the armrests of her chair. She was in the back this time. She wouldn't be so scared. Would she?

Her heart lurched as the plane raced down the runway and leaped gracefully into the air. She forced herself to let go of the armrest long enough to remove an airsick bag from the seat pocket. She might need it. As her stomach lurched again, she suddenly remembered her date with Scott. She hadn't called . . . or even had time to leave a note. Still, this was Coorah Creek. She was sure someone would tell him what was happening.

The plane bounced as it hit an air pocket and all thoughts of Scott left Katie's head. Her only concern now was trying not to throw up.

15

This wasn't how he'd planned to spend his evening. Scott took another swig on his beer and glared along the bar at the Christmas tree, shining and sparkling away with no regard for his mood. Bah Humbug!

For a few minutes he contemplated going and getting his laptop. He could answer some e-mails, or even hunt for a place to live in England. There were plenty of things he should be doing. But what he really wanted was to be in Katie's tiny flat, watching her as she cooked, waiting for the smile that lit not just her face, but the whole room. He wanted to listen to her voice. They never seemed to run out of things to talk about, but what he loved most of all was just the sound of her voice. That cute accent had somehow worked its way into his heart and lodged there. A day without Katie in it was not a good day.

And there it was — his real problem.

He was going to leave Coorah Creek very soon.

His aim in coming here was to see his father. If he'd hoped for some sort of rapprochement — it hadn't happened. But at least some contact had been made. All he had to do now was tell his father about his job in England, and leave.

But that also meant leaving Katie — and in his heart of hearts, he didn't want to do that. Just his luck to meet someone like her in the one place on Earth where he would never live again. And just as she was starting to make a home and a life here.

The lights on the Christmas tree twinkled at him, and he scowled again.

Bah humbug indeed!

'So, are you planning to sit here glaring at that inoffensive tree all night, or do you want to make yourself useful?'

Scott turned to look at Trish. She was at her usual place behind the bar doing her usual thing — getting involved in everyone else's business. He grunted in a non-committal sort of way, but she was totally unaffected.

'Excellent. Some of the men are down at the church hall, getting ready for the Waifs and Orphans on Christmas Day. They could use an extra hand.'

'Waifs and Orphans?'

'It started a few years ago, when the mine was just opening. All the people without families got together on Christmas day. It started here in the pub — but it's grown bigger and now half the town comes. We moved it to the hall a couple of years ago.'

'So am I a waif or an orphan?' he asked, his mood not improved one whit.

'That's entirely up to you,' Trish said, her smile never faltering. 'You don't have to be either, unless you want to be.'

Her eyes were far too knowing as she

stared him down.

Admitting defeat, Scott tossed back the last of his beer and slid off his stool. At least it would stop him thinking about Katie off somewhere on a rescue mission. 'So, where do I go?'

Scott remembered the Church. As a kid, he'd been there once or twice, but there hadn't been enough people for a permanent minister of any denomination. Services had been held at odd intervals whenever a churchman was passing through. Times had changed now. He had spotted at least one other church in the town, and both had looked prosperous. The hall was a recent addition. A long wooden building with a corrugated iron roof that was already showing signs of rust. The weather out here was quick to take its toll.

There were several cars parked outside. Scott slipped his into line beside them and headed for the open doors of the hall, his mood starting to lift at the thought of doing something useful. The hall was surprisingly large and bright. At one end of the hall, dark red curtains had been pushed back to reveal a small wooden stage. No doubt the local school kids had performed many a play there. The place was buzzing with activity. He wasn't the only one Trish had bullied into helping. He saw Jack North, her sometime barman, struggling to drag a heavy cast iron bathtub out from under the stage. That bathtub would no doubt be filled with ice on Christmas morning to keep the beer cold.

In one corner of the room, a couple of women were pulling decorations out of a couple of big cardboard boxes. The boxes were dusty, the tinsel glinted in the strong overhead lights as they sorted the red, green and gold into separate piles. He could see other women through a door to his left. They were in what appeared to be a kitchen doing whatever mysterious things were done in kitchens before large parties. Further towards the back of the hall, another door was open. As Scott watched, one of the working party emerged holding one end of a long broad piece of wood; the makings of a table no doubt.

This was not Christmas as Scott had ever known it. Christmas had never been a time of laughter and sharing. Not for many many years. He started to cross the pale wooden floor. Then another sound stopped him dead.

A man was laughing. It was a sound he hadn't heard in a very long time — but he knew it in an instant.

He turned slowly to see Ed carrying an empty oil drum from the back room. The drum still bore the hint of last year's festive decorations. Ed was obviously sharing a joke with the man working with him. He looked younger. He looked happy. He looked . . . not at all like the Ed Collins who Scott hated.

★   ★   ★

Ed put the drum down in front of the stage. At some point in the next few days, a tree would be placed in there

158

— with sand to hold it firm. Then would come the decorations. For the first time in many years, Ed decided he was looking forward to Christmas Day. Especially if Trish was right about Scott.

He turned around and looked down the hall, straight into his son's face.

'It's looking good,' Scott said to the room in general, but his eyes never left his father's face.

Ed didn't hesitate. Still smiling he walked towards his son. This was an opportunity. It might be the last and he wasn't going to waste it.

'I think it'll be all right come Christmas Day,' Ed said. 'But there's still a lot of work to do.'

'I came to help. What do you need me to do?'

'Ellen is giving the orders,' Ed said, motioning towards a small blonde woman who was sorting decorations. 'Let's see what she needs.'

'Decorations have to go on the beams,' Ellen told them. There's a ladder in the back room.

'Yes, Ma'am,' Ed bowed slightly. 'And exactly how do you want them arranged?'

'You are two big strong men,' Ellen slapped Ed's arm gently and smiled at Scott. 'I'm sure the two of you can figure it out.'

'Yes, Ma'am,' Scott aped his father's bow. Father and son exchanged a glance, and hesitantly they both smiled.

They worked together for about an hour. Ed held the ladder while Scott climbed to the rafters to drape tinsel over and along the beams. There were colourful paper lanterns to be added, and spinning paper balls. Any tension between them slowly faded. They didn't talk much, but Ed didn't mind. He was more than content with what they had. Around them, other workers were laying out the trestle tables and wiping away the dust that had gathered since they were last used.

'All right — who needs a beer and a burger?'

Trish and Syd Warren walked through the door clutching boxes. Ed moved to take Trish's load and she gave him a knowing smile as she handed the box over. The beer and burgers were good. Ed enjoyed the camaraderie and for the first time found himself thinking that he had spent far too much time alone with his bitterness and regrets. He realised now that his isolation from the townsfolk has been his own fault. Most of the newer townsfolk didn't know about his past. Most of the long-time residents didn't care. It had taken the return of his son to show him what had always been in front of him.

The working party disposed of the burgers and beer in no time at all and began to break up. Ed walked out into the night and stretched his back. As he did, he looked up into a sky glittering with stars.

'I missed those stars when I moved to the city,' Scott said as he came to stand beside his father. 'There's nowhere on earth with stars like these.'

'There must have been stars back east,' Ed said.

'Yes. But they weren't like this.'

They stood in silence for a few minutes more.

'I'm heading back,' Scott said. 'Do you need a lift?'

'Well, I kinda like walking at night.'

'Do you want some company?'

'Yeah.'

Scott put his car keys back in his pocket and the two of them set out. It wasn't going to take long to walk back. After two or three minutes, Scott broke the silence.

'I opened a workshop you know.'

'Did you?'

'Yeah. I restore old classic cars. I'm pretty good at it too.'

Ed smiled in the darkness, a feeling of pride growing inside him. Despite everything, his son had become a good man. 'Well, as a boy you always loved those old cars. You had dozens of books about them.'

'I sure did.'

'There're all still there you know. In your old room. You should come and get them.'

There was a long silence. Ed knew what Scott didn't say. That he didn't want to return to the house where he had experienced so much unhappiness. Ed couldn't blame him for that.

'I've been offered a job,' Scott said at last, 'restoring, among other things, a Lancia Aurelia and a 1956 Mercedes Gullwing.'

Ed let out a low whistle. 'There aren't many of those around.'

'There aren't.'

Scott hesitated and Ed knew there was something important about to be said.

'Not in this country. The job is in England. At the National Museum of Motoring.'

Ed's long stride faltered just a fraction, but he kept walking without looking at his son. 'Ah. That explains why you were looking at their website the other night. That's quite something.

You'll enjoy that. When do you leave?'

'I was supposed to go this week, but I thought I might stay a bit longer. Trish has invited me to join the party and as I've put in the work . . . ' His voice trailed off.

'It will be good to have you here for Christmas.'

They were almost back at the pub. Ed was about to suggest that Scott and he stop for a last beer, when movement up ahead caught his eye.

'Candy?'

The old Labrador was limping slowly towards them, her tail wagging.

'Hey, what are you doing out?' Ed dropped to one knee to pat the dog. Candy's tail waved happily, and she included Scott in the adoring gaze she cast at Ed. 'That old gate doesn't shut properly anymore,' Ed said as he stood. 'I'll get on that in the morning. She shouldn't be out on the road.'

Scott nodded his agreement.

'I'd better take her back.' Ed rose to his feet. After a moment's hesitation, he held out his hand. 'Goodnight, Son.'

Scott took it. 'Goodnight, Dad.'

As they shook, Ed realised this was the first time he had touched his son since that last night. The night he had lifted his fist to a heartbroken and angry boy. The sense of shame he now felt was overpowering. He wanted to say something. To apologise and ask for Scott's forgiveness. But instead, he turned and, with his dog at his side, crossed the road back to his dark and empty house.

16

'It's all right you know. There's nothing to be ashamed off.'

Katie splashed some more water over her face.

'Some people just don't like small planes,' Jess's voice continued from the other side of the bathroom door. 'Really. I have a pilot friend who throws up if he gets into anything smaller than a 747.'

Katie appreciated Jess's good intentions, but right now, nothing was going to make her feel any better. She rinsed her mouth out again, then wiped her face on the towel. From the mirror, a white-faced woman looked back at her, her eyes rimmed with red. It wasn't a very flattering image. She turned away.

Jess was waiting outside. The hangar doors were wide open. So was the door to the air ambulance. Jess was carrying a bucket.

'I'll clean it up,' Katie said, her cheeks burning at the thought of what Jess was about to do.

'Don't worry. I'll do it.' Jess put a comforting hand on her shoulder. 'It's an air ambulance remember. I've had to clean up far worse.'

Katie wanted to insist. Perhaps salvage just a little bit of self-respect. But the thought of climbing back inside that plane was almost enough to make her retch again.

'Thank you,' she said in a whisper.

'It's not a problem.' Jess hesitated. 'You know, some people just aren't cut out for . . . this.' She waved an arm that seemed to encompass everything from the tin shed that was her hanger, to the aircraft and the whole of the outback. 'I'm not trying to get rid of you or anything. And Adam says you're a good nurse. But maybe . . . just maybe this isn't the right place for you.'

That thought had already occurred to Katie. And she had trouble shaking it as she drove back towards the hospital and her small flat. It would be so easy to simply go home. Jess and Adam would understand why. And her family would too, when she arrived back in London. No-one would blame her. Well, no-one but herself. To leave now would be to admit that she had failed. Failed to prove to herself that nursing was the right place for her. Failed to recapture her passion for the only career she had ever wanted. And if she gave up now, what would she do? Get a job stacking shelves in a supermarket? Maybe she could get a job at a school. That wasn't what she wanted.

Feeling pretty despondent she turned into the hospital driveway — and saw Scott. He was sitting on the hospital veranda, obviously waiting for her. Her heart did a little somersault.

There was another reason not to pack up and go home. Scott. As a nurse she'd been chatted up by more than a few doctors. She'd been taken out to dinner in fancy restaurants with fine wine. And not one of them had ever made her heart leap like that.

What was it about this man sitting on her doorstep with a bag that no doubt contained beer? In just a few days he had come to mean more to her than any of those smart doctors with their fancy restaurants and expensive wine.

Realisation crashed down on her like a block of concrete. She didn't want to leave Coorah Creek because she didn't want to leave Scott. Yet Scott was going to leave too.

She didn't believe in love at first sight. Attraction — yes. Lust — of course. And there was certainly a fair measure of both between her and Scott. Not love. Not yet. But maybe if they gave themselves a chance, this could become something special.

But Scott was leaving. All she would have is a job she didn't really enjoy. Jess was right. Coorah Creek was not the place for her.

She parked the car, and almost before she was out, Scott was at her side.

'How are you feeling?'

She frowned. 'I'm fine.'

'Trish said you'd been sick on the plane.'

'How does that woman know these things?' Katie shook her head. 'Is she psychic? Does she have CCTV cameras all over town? How does she do it?'

Scott chuckled, and wrapped his arms around her in a mighty bear hug.

He doesn't care, she thought, that I have been sick on the plane. I hate to think what I smell like. And god knows I look awful. But he doesn't care about that. He cares about me. Me.

And suddenly she really did feel fine. Even better than fine.

By the time she had showered and changed, Scott had a cup of tea waiting for her. They settled on her couch and Katie felt herself begin to relax. She told Scott about the flight to help a stockman who had fallen from a windmill while fixing it, and broken his arm.

'It was a nasty break. But Adam fixed

it,' she said. 'He's a good doctor. He does things on site that would require transport to a hospital back home.' She sighed heavily.

'I hope that sigh wasn't caused by our handsome doctor,' Scott joked.

'No,' Katie grinned. 'I was just thinking — '

'What?'

'When I was younger I wanted to be a doctor. I imagined myself being some sort of hero and saving lives. Doing the sort of thing Adam does almost every day.'

'Why didn't you?'

'I don't come from an affluent family. They wouldn't have been able to afford to put me through medical school. None of the kids at my school ever aimed that high. I was lucky to be able to study nursing.'

'Any regrets?'

'Sometimes. Nursing in a big London hospital isn't really for me. It's too impersonal. The patients all run together into a blur. There are times I felt I wasn't really helping anyone.'

'So it's better for you here?'

'The work is better. But the flying terrifies me. I doubt I will ever be able to do the air ambulance thing properly.'

'You'll get used to it,' Scott said.

'Either that or I'll have to get some better travel sickness pills. The ones Adam gave me today didn't help at all.'

Scott lifted her hand and gently kissed the back of it. 'You'll figure it out. I have faith in you.'

At that moment, as she looked into his smiling eyes and waited for him to kiss her lips, she believed him.

* * *

It was quite a few minutes before Scott was able to stop kissing Katie. He just loved the softness of her lips. He could go on kissing her for hours. He could do a lot more too, but he wasn't going to. It was going to be hard enough to leave her now. If this thing between them went any further, he would never want to walk away.

'I spent some time with my dad last night,' he said.

Her face lit up. 'That's great. What did you do?'

'It was that woman again.' He grinned. 'Trish roped me into helping them to set up for the town Christmas party. Dad was there. We worked together for a bit.'

'Are you starting to mend the bridges?'

'I think so. We walked back together afterwards and we talked.'

'What did you talk about?'

It had come. He'd told his father. Now it was time to tell Katie.

'I have a job offer. Restoring classic cars for a motor museum.'

'Wonderful! That sounds just right for you. Tell me all about it.'

She was looking at him, her eyes shining with joy for him. But what would happen if he told her that the job was in England? He couldn't do it. It was wrong, he knew that, but he wanted to postpone that moment as long as possible.

He wouldn't lie to her, but at this moment, he just couldn't tell her the truth.

'I met the manager when he came into my shop. He liked the work I was doing. They have two amazing new cars arriving soon. Really rare and valuable. He offered me the job restoring them. It's an honour really.'

'That's great! We should celebrate. I can make that dinner I promised you last night before I got called away.' Katie was getting to her feet. He reached out to pull her back to the couch.

'Wait. Katie. I . . . I'm thinking of saying no.'

'Oh.'

She sat beside him, looking at his face. He could see the question in her eyes.

'The job would mean leaving Coorah Creek. There are a lot of things holding me here,' he said. 'I think I am starting to make some connection with Dad . . . '

'That's great,' she said softly. 'I'm happy for you.'

'And there's you, Katie. I don't want

to leave just yet. I want to spend more time with you. I've never felt this close to anyone before. And so quickly. I don't know what it is . . . or what it might become. But I'm not ready to walk away. Not yet.'

He saw the tears in her eyes, adding to their luminous shine. Gently he reached out to run his thumb along her cheekbone. It came back damp.

'I don't want you to.'

He kissed her. Her tears added a spicy saltiness to the softness of her lips. He took her face between the palms of his hands, and kissed those tears away. Then they kissed some more, long deep slow kisses that drove the sadness away.

'You know,' Katie said with a smile when at last they could both speak again. 'You are my oldest friend in this whole country. Not by much,' she added hastily. 'I only met you half an hour before I met some of the other people here. But that half hour; it means a lot when you're a long way from home at Christmas.'

He heard the pain underneath the words. She was homesick. He understood that. He would do everything he could to drive that away. He wrapped his arms around her and pulled her close and as he did he realised something strange. If she was his oldest friend — her second oldest friend — the second person she had met in The Creek — was his father. Maybe there was a lesson there . . . but he had no idea what it was.

17

The rain on the roof sounded as if all the dwarves from Middle Earth were up there pounding away with their hammers, and had brought their friends from Snow White along for the ride. The ceaseless pounding on the corrugated iron roof was deafening. Katie put her hands over her ears. After a couple of weeks of rising temperatures and brilliant blue skies, the wet season had arrived with a vengeance.

She turned over and covered her head with her pillow.

What sort of a country only had two seasons? Back in England, the changing of the seasons was accompanied by soft changes in light, by leaf kicking and pristine white snow. There were brilliant summer days, punctuated by bird song, and cold wet winter nights to spend huddled in front of a roaring fire. You knew where you where weather-wise in England.

But not here. Oh no!

There were no leaves to kick — because those scrubby gum trees never lost their leaves. There was no winter . . . only a wet season and a dry season — differentiated, thusly by one wit at the pub: during the dry season it's hot all the time and doesn't rain and in the wet season it's hot all the time and rains almost every day. Call that seasons? She certainly didn't.

She sat up in bed and glared at the ceiling — as if by doing so she could stop the rain. The drumming continued.

Katie slid out of bed and padded barefoot into the living room. She walked over to the window and stared out at the rain. There wasn't much to see. Without street lights or a light from another building, it was too dark. Sighing, she made her way to the kitchen and flicked the kettle on. Tea would help. It always did.

As she waited for the water to boil, she glanced at the clock. It was just after 11 o'clock. Almost Christmas Day. And she felt about as Christmassy as a cold cheese and tomato sandwich.

She poured the tea and walked back into her lounge room. The steam rising from her cup served to highlight the temperature as she went to switch on the overhead fan. Christmas shouldn't be in mid-summer. It just didn't feel right to have Christmas with not even the faintest hope of a snowball.

She blew across the top of her cup to cool the liquid, and took a small sip. Her mum always said a good cup of tea made every situation better. She was probably right . . . she was about most things. Oh, but Katie missed her family. Especially now. If she was back in England, she would be at her parents' house, with her brother and sister. They'd be drinking tea too — but doing it together. And talking.

A fierce crack of lightning caused her to jump. Damn this storm. Not only was it keeping her awake, her somewhat fragile internet connection had given up the ghost. She'd only managed about two minutes of Skype conversation with her family earlier this evening, before the connection dropped out. God only knew when it would come back.

She sipped her tea again and admitted that really, she was just in a bad mood. Totally homesick. And lonely.

It wasn't just that her family weren't here. She was missing the whole Christmas experience. She hadn't even wrapped a present. Sure, she'd sent some small souvenirs home to her family — but that wasn't the same as piling brightly wrapped gifts, covered in ribbons and bows under a tree. She didn't have anyone to wrap a present for.

Except Scott.

She so wanted to give Scott a gift. Somehow, in all the strangeness of this new life, he was the one thing that felt familiar and comforting. That felt like home. She'd taken some time off work and scoured every shop in Coorah Creek for a present. There were not many shops, and nothing that she wanted to give to Scott. Sure, she could buy him a bottle of wine, or a new hat. But she wanted something a bit more personal than that. Something that would let him know she would miss him when he was gone back to the city for his new job. She wanted a gift that would tell him how wonderful it was to have him in a place that was so strange there were times she wasn't even sure she spoke the same language. Language! That was it.

She leaped to her feet. At her going away party, her friends had given her gifts. The usual joke gifts that suited such occasions. She found what she was looking for in a drawer in her bedroom. It was a book — The English-Australian Dictionary. She flicked through the pages as she carried it back to the couch. There were the usual entries — Sheila as Australian for girl. Bonza meaning good — although she'd not heard any

Australian actually say that. There were some interesting words too. She didn't know that a wild horse was called a brumby in Australia. And that the peppers she ate in the UK were called capsicums in the southern hemisphere.

She found a pen and notebook and started scribbling down words . . . ridgy-didge (genuine), cobber (friend) Pommy (English person) . . . there was a lot of material. She chewed the end of the pen and tried a few phrases on the notebook. She was getting there. At last she had it figured out. She turned to the front page of the phrase book and began to write. The last word caused her to pause. She flicked through the book one more time, but some words are the same in every language.

When she was done, she pulled out a map of Queensland she had bought on her first day in the country. Coorah Creek was circled in black felt pen. That would make great wrapping paper.

At last the gift was ready. It wasn't anything like any Christmas gift she had wrapped before. There were no ribbons and bows. No red and green and gold fancy paper. It wasn't the most expensive she'd ever given either. But this gift was as personal to her as a gift could be.

She sat back and yawned. The blinking clock on her TV showed that it was ten minutes past midnight. Christmas Day! Not only that, the room was silent. She hadn't noticed that the rain had stopped. A good thing too, she thought, or else Santa and his reindeer would get wet. Or did kangaroos pull Santa's sleigh in this part of the world.

Smiling, she made her way back to bed. Her last thought as she fell asleep was that maybe this wasn't going to be such a bad 'Chrissy' after all.

18

Christmas morning dawned bright and sunny at Coorah Creek. The trees still shone with the last drops of the overnight rain and the air had that crisp clean taste that only comes after a thunderstorm. The kookaburras fluffed their feathers and chortled as the sun rose. A lone kangaroo hopped across the road on the outskirts of town, and disappeared in the direction of the national park to the north. The huge machinery of the mine was silent on this one day of the year when no work was done.

In her bedroom, Katie slept on, her curtains shut to preserve the cool darkness for as long as possible. The map-wrapped package lay on the coffee table, next to the mug she had failed to wash the night before.

In their nearby house, Adam and Jess

were still in bed, but not asleep. Their Christmas had started early with an exchange of gifts and a champagne breakfast in bed.

As always, Ed Collins was out of bed with the sun. His first task this Christmas morning, as it was every day, was to pat the dog, and let her out. Candy wagged her tail as she began her slow and careful descent of the stairs from the back door to the garden. Watching her struggle, Ed felt sadness steal over him. She was so very old. According to the vet, she wasn't in any pain, but Ed knew he wouldn't have her company for much longer. He looked across the road to the pub, where his son was sleeping. He wouldn't have Scott for very much longer either.

Inside the pub, Trish and Syd were also up and about. As the prime movers behind the Waifs and Orphans party, there was a lot for them to do. Trish and Syd didn't exchange Christmas gifts any more. Their Christmas was all about other people. Deep down, Trish knew this was their way of dealing with the fact that they had never been blessed with children. But she had long since come to terms with that. As long as there were people in the world she could help, she was content.

And speaking of helping . . . She heard movement in the room just above her kitchen. If Scott and his father didn't sort themselves out soon, she'd do more than give them a gentle nudge in the right direction. In fact, she could probably start today. But, to be fair, she would cook the boy a good breakfast first. He deserved that much.

★ ★ ★

The smell of cooking greeted Scott as he came down the stairs. And not just the normal breakfast smells of coffee and bacon. He walked into the kitchen to find Trish hard at work.

'Merry Christmas.' He risked giving her a quick peck on the cheek and was rewarded with a smile. She wasn't such a bad sort, he thought as he helped himself to coffee.

'Tuck into this,' Trish said as she slid a plate onto the table. 'There's a lot of work to do to get ready for the Waifs and Orphans.'

'Yes, Ma'am.'

'Are you planning to go over the road this morning?'

'I'll see my father at the party.' Scott kept his voice casual. He had thought about going to visit his father . . . but had decided against it. He had no gift to give him. He had no idea what he could even say. They had barely acknowledged Christmas when Scott was a boy . . . it would seem strange to make a fuss now.

Trish said nothing, but the way she did it spoke volumes.

By the time Scott had finished his breakfast, Trish was starting to pack food and ice into several huge coolers.

'If you're ready,' Trish said in a voice that brooked no denial, 'I need you to take a load of chairs to the hall. After that, there's ice in the freezer in the bar. And all this food is just about ready to go too. You'd better use our ute. You can take bigger loads in that.'

'I'm on it.'

He wasn't the only one. By the time he had driven to the hall, the back of the ute piled high with chairs and stools, there were already several cars there. He grabbed the first load and walked up the stairs. He took one step inside the hall and stopped, feeling his mouth drop open.

The scene in front of him was all the Christmas dreams he'd ever had as a child. It was his first memories of Christmas, when his mother was still with him and the house was filled with colour and life and love. It was everything he had lost when she left. Everything his father had never allowed in those long dark years.

The hall was dripping with decorations. Although Scott had helped with some of the work, this was the first time he's seen them in their full glory.

Someone had installed a tree at one end of the hall and it glittered with colour and light. Lights had also been strung along the timber beams above his head, adding an extra layer of sparkle to the already dazzling room. The tables he had helped to arrange were now covered with cloth — the wide range of size and colour and pattern was testament to the fact that they had come from many different homes. So too had the assortment of plates and glasses stacked ready for the start of the party. On some of the tables, there were vases of flowers; a rare sight in this dry and dusty place. There still weren't many chairs, but he was about to change that.

'Hey, the chairs are here,' a voice called from the back of the room. Several men came forward to help unload the back of his vehicle, wishing him a merry Christmas as they did. The back of the ute was empty in no time at all, and Scott returned to the pub for the next load. Once again many hands helped make light of the unloading. The crowd was growing now. Families walked through the door, calling greetings to their neighbours. Kids were showing off their presents to anyone who might listen. It seemed every family brought something to add to the party. A home baked cake. A bowl of potato salad or a ham. Beer and soft drink was pushed into the ice in the bathtubs along one wall. Then someone turned on the music. As the first Christmas carol filled the air, Scott glanced at the doorway to see his father walk in.

Ed looked like a different person. His greasy overalls had been exchanged for blue jeans and a crisp white cotton shirt. It wasn't just that he looked clean — he looked less worn down by care. Younger too. He crossed the room to where Scott was standing. For a few moments, the two of them just stood there, both not sure what to say or do.

'Merry Christmas, Dad.'

This was what he had come back to

Coorah Creek to do. Scott held out his hand. The last time he and his father had touched, their hands had been fists.

All around them, people were hugging and laughing and exchanging gifts.

Ed reached out and took Scott's hand. 'Merry Christmas, Son.'

19

Katie was running late for the party. Her morning had been thrown out by the arrival of a couple of patients at the hospital. She'd helped Adam set the broken arm of a child who had become too adventurous on the swing set he'd been given for Christmas. And she'd dressed a burn on a woman's hand which was good argument against too much champagne at breakfast before lighting the barbecue for Christmas lunch. She would Skype her family back in England when the time differences allowed, so she had set off to the Waifs and Orphans party — where she had already arranged to meet Scott.

The hall was humming when she arrived. Music was wafting through the open doors and windows, as was the sound of talk and laughter. When she entered the hall, Katie stopped and looked around her. The old wooden hall had been changed into a wonderland. It was Christmas in all its glory . . . but so different as to be almost unrecognisable.

The tree that glowed so brightly at the end of the hall was like no other Christmas tree she had ever seen. No tall stately pine, this tree was as broad as it was high. A profusion of branches spread from multiple trunks, the long broad dark green leaves drooping towards the floor. The tree sported as much tinsel and as many lights as anyone could hope for — but the snow in its branches was just cotton wool.

In England, her Christmas had always been marked by a roaring log fire, the flickering firelight adding to the warmth of the room. Not so in Coorah Creek. The room was already hot. There were no woolly scarves or bright Christmas knits. Shorts and T-shirts seemed to be the dress code for most of the party goers. However there was, she was pleased to see, a smattering of Santa hats.

The room was brilliantly decorated with tinsel and shining glass balls. There were hand-made cut out stars, no doubt produced at the school. There were brightly wrapped boxes under the tree. The tables were almost groaning under the weight of the food that was laid out. But Katie would not call it a proper Christmas lunch. There were huge bowls of salad and fruit. She spied buckets of fresh prawns — although how they came to be so far from the ocean she wasn't sure. There were legs of ham cooked on the bone, the thick skin peeled back to reveal the succulent meat beneath. There was ice-cream stored, like the beer, in tubs of ice. There was turkey — or perhaps it was chicken — but it was cold and laid out alongside other cold meats.

Where was the steaming roast and stuffing? The rich dark pudding and the mince pies? Not to mentioned the roast potatoes and the bread sauce? And where oh where was the gravy? The thick tasty gravy that her mother always made with white wine and just a touch of mustard to give it extra bite.

This wasn't Christmas as she knew it, but the room did exude the gaiety and joy she was looking for. Many of the faces were unknown to her — but even this far from her home, the smiles were the same. And in the midst of it all, totally recognisable and drawing her to him like a homing pigeon to its nest, was Scott.

He was laughing at something someone had just said. He was dressed simply in blue jeans and a T-shirt, but she had never seen any man look so good, as he tossed his head back and laughed again. Even amid the hubbub of noise around her, she could hear his laugh as clearly as if he was standing next to her. He looked so at ease here in the midst of this very summery Christmas, with these people from whom he had run all those years ago. He stopped laughing and turned around, almost as if he could feel her eyes on him. When he saw her, his face lit up. He excused himself and hurried towards her.

'Katie. Merry Christmas.'

'Merry — '

Before she could finish the greeting, Scott had taken her in his arms and kissed her. For a few seconds, all she was aware of was how good it felt in his arms. With his lips on hers. How right it felt. And suddenly, the strangeness of this Christmas Day was gone. In some deep and unexplained way, here in a place she had seen for the first time such a short time ago, she had come home.

When Scott finally released her, she was astounded to hear whistles and cheering and catcalls. She looked around at the smiling faces of the townsfolk, and blushed to the very tip of her toes.

'Come on,' Scott said. 'I'll get you a drink.'

By mid-afternoon, the party was in full swing. People came and went as they wished. The food and drink flowed in what seemed a never ending abundance. Katie smiled to see Trish and Syd Warren moving through the crowds, playing the role of hosts although, in truth, the town itself was the host on this occasion. Adam and Jess were there, as was Ken Travers, the storeowner and her patient. His wife was with him and a teenage girl she assumed was their daughter. Jack North was playing Santa for a group of kids — a couple of which she believed were his. There were people she didn't know, but she guessed that by the end of the day, no-one in that room would be a stranger any more.

Katie felt a warm glow, and she wasn't certain if it was caused by the soaring temperature, the delicious if somewhat alcoholic fruit punch being served from a huge bowl, or Scott, who was never far from her side, his voice and honest laughter punctuating her day. Whenever possible his hand found hers, although that wasn't too often given their need to distribute food and drink and to constantly embrace both children and adults.

Scott was off collecting another load of ice from the pub freezer, when his father sought Katie out.

'Merry Christmas,' he said.

'And to you too,' she said, meaning it.

'Having Scott here has made this the best Christmas in a very long time,' Ed said. 'I know you have helped too.'

'I haven't done anything.'

'Yes, you have. You've been a friend to him. Given him someone to talk to. And I know you have been encouraging him to try to overcome the bad feeling that's been between us all these years.'

'He set out to do that long before he met me,' Katie said.

'I know. But you've helped him . . . us. I wanted to thank you for that.'

Katie felt herself blushing again.

'My son cares for you,' Ed said matter-of-factly.

'I care for him too.'

At that moment, Scott re-entered the

building carrying a huge bag of crushed ice. To the cheers of the crowd, he up-ended the ice into the big bathtub full of beer, sending water splashing over the sides. Amid much back-slapping, he accepted another beer from one of the men.

'So, are you having a good time?' he asked Katie as he re-joined her.

'Yes. I was feeling really homesick this morning, but I'm not any more.' She gave his hand a squeeze to let him know how much he was responsible for the improvement in her day.

'Scott,' Ed spoke hesitantly. 'I have a couple of things at the house that . . . That I thought you might like to have. If you could come over.'

'What things?'

'It's better that you come and take a look. It could be now. Or later if you would prefer.'

Scott glanced at Katie, a question in his eyes. She could feel his hesitation. He had declared his intention never to set foot in his father's house again. But things were changing and she knew this was something he had to do.

'Go,' she said without hesitation.

'Will you . . . '

'I'll be fine. I promised Trish I would take care of the next round of washing up. Then I need to head back anyway. The time will be right to Skype my family back home.'

'Can I come over to your place later?'

'You'd better. I have something for you too.'

20

They walked back towards the garage in silence. Ed found it a little hard to believe that after all these years, Scott was coming back to the house they had once both called home. This was a chance for a new start, but Ed didn't know how to make it work. There were some things he should give to Scott, but that wasn't his only reasons for inviting his son back to the house. He still harboured a hope that if Scott could walk back through that front door, some of the pain of the past few years might wash away.

As they approached the darkened buildings on the corner of the town's main street, Ed found he was looking at his home and business with new eyes. Through Scott's eyes. Both buildings were shabby and in need of new paint. The garden, if you could call it that, was overgrown and wild. The grime that went with his business had slowly spread to cover his whole life. And this was how Scott had lived as a boy. He hadn't been a very good father to his son. It was a wonder that Scott had grown into the man he was.

They reached the rusty side gate. Ed automatically looked for movement in the overgrown garden; the flash of gold and accompanying bark that would tell them Candy had noticed their arrival. For a long time now, she had been the only one to greet his return at the end of each day. Without her the loneliness would have been even harder to bear.

There was no movement in the garden. Ed opened the gate, a frown starting to form on his forehead.

'Candy. Where are you girl?'

There was no answer. Ed walked towards the house, pushing aside the branches of an overgrowing bush. Then he saw her.

'Oh, no. Candy.' The softly spoken words were torn from the depth of Ed's soul.

The Labrador was lying on her side near the steps leading to his back door. Her legs were caught under her body as if she had fallen while trying to climb the stairs. Her eyes were closed and her tongue lolled from her open mouth. She was still breathing, but every slow laboured breath seemed as if it would be her last. Ed knelt by her head and ran his hand over her muzzle. When she stirred slightly and licked his fingers, his heart almost broke.

He heard Scott come up behind him.

'Help me get her inside.'

Scott hurried up the steps. The door wasn't locked. He opened it and stepped aside to allow Ed to carry the dog through. Ed carried his old friend through to the living room, and lowered her very gently onto a much used dog bed that sat beside his old armchair.

Ed crouched beside her, stroking her head gently. Scott joined him. Candy opened her eyes and stared up at the two men. Slowly the very tip of her tail began to wag. Just a little. She licked

Scott's fingers as he reached out to stroke her, then her eyes closed again.

'Should I go and find the vet?' Scott asked.

Ed shook his head. 'We knew this was coming. She's just old. Too old.' His voice broke. The hands that reached out to stroke the old dog's head were shaking.

The three of them stayed like that for what seemed a very long time. After each breath Candy took, Scott and Ed waited an eternity until she took the next. When, at last she didn't, the room seemed very very silent.

Grief crashed down on Ed like a physical thing. His only friend was gone. He felt so terribly alone. For the first time in many long years, tears began to stream down his face. He looked at Scott and saw the same grief in his eyes. It was as if time had shifted and Scott was a boy again, looking to him for comfort when his mother left. Ed had failed his son then. And he was terribly afraid he would fail again.

Both men rose to their feet. For the first time since they'd entered, Scott looked around him. Ed knew the room hadn't changed much in the last eight years. The furniture was older. Shabbier. But Scott would recognise his home.

He knew the moment Scott saw the photograph. His body stiffened. He walked over to the bookshelf and lifted the silver frame from its place. Inside that frame was a photo of a beautiful young woman and a small boy.

'I thought you threw everything away,' Scott said slowly.

'No. I just put them away. After you left, I wanted something . . . ' Ed couldn't continue.

Scott turned around. His face, still wet tears, was contorted with grief and anger.

'Why? Why did you do it?'

Ed didn't answer.

'She was beautiful. She was a wonderful wife and mother. And you had an affair! Why did you do that?

Why did you drive her away?'

Ed struggled to find the words he needed, but they wouldn't come. He saw the disgust spread over Scott's face. He put the photo back on the bookshelf and turned to walk out of the room, away from this house and his father. Ed knew that if his son left, he would never see him again.

His throat contracted. The words were too hard to speak.

'It wasn't me.'

*   *   *

The words stopped Scott in his tracks, but he didn't turn around. 'What do you mean it wasn't you?'

'I didn't have the affair. She did.'

At first, Scott thought he'd misheard. But he hadn't. His father's voice had never been clearer or more firm.

'You're lying.'

'No. For the first time, I am telling the truth.'

Slowly Scott turned to face his

206

father, still unwilling to believe what he'd heard.

'Why should I believe you?' Ed had given him no reason to trust him, and every reason to walk away.

'After everything that has happened, why would I lie now?'

Scott studied his father's face. The pain in his eyes told Scott that this time he was hearing the truth. He felt as if his whole world was shaking beneath him.

'Why didn't you tell me? All those years ago. Why did you lie then?'

'I needed it to be a secret. I wanted to believe . . . ' Ed blinked back the tears. 'I wanted to believe she'd come back. I had to believe she'd come back. And when she did, I didn't want her to be the subject of town gossip. If they had to blame someone — if you had to blame someone — I wanted it to be me.'

'And that last day, you let me fight you, and then walk away without knowing the truth.'

'You said you were going to look for her. I wanted you to find her. And if you did, the two of you had to be all right together. It would be better if you both blamed me. And, I guess I still hoped there was a chance for me.'

'That she would come back to you?'

'That you both would.'

Scott shook his head, trying to make sense of what he was hearing. Years of anger and bitterness and hate had been based on a lie.

'I know better now,' Ed said in a very quiet voice. 'She was never going to come back to me. She had the affair, but it was as much my fault as hers. I am not an easy man to live with.'

'No. You're not.'

'Scott, I am so sorry.' Ed's voice cracked with the weight of years of loneliness and regret. 'You are so like her, you know. Now and then. Every time I looked at you, I saw her in your eyes. I couldn't stand the pain, so I guess I stopped looking at you. Stopped seeing you. It was the only way I could survive.'

A long moment passed, broken only by the sound of their breathing. Scott looked into his father's face and saw love there. There was fear, too. He was afraid that Scott would walk away again.

Scott reached deep inside his own heart. He'd come back to Coorah Creek looking for answers. Tonight, he'd found them.

They both moved at the same time. In the middle of the room, Ed threw his arms around his son and pulled him into his chest. They held each other for a long moment. When they broke apart, there were tears in both their eyes.

'I have some of her things still,' Ed said. 'I thought you might like something to remember her by. She left me — but she always loved you.'

'And you have always loved her?'

'Son, I fell in love with your mother the day I met her. I'm not entirely sure I have ever stopped loving her.'

'I loved her so much when I was a boy. I tried to find her. I really did. I checked electoral rolls. I posted messages all over the internet and took out ads in newspapers. I used to wonder if she saw them and just didn't want to see me. I can hardly remember her now. Would it hurt you to talk about her?'

'No. I'd welcome the chance to talk. I thought you'd never come back either. I did try to find you . . . but I didn't think you would want to see me.'

'I didn't then, but things change. People change.'

'They do.' Ed took a deep breath and pulled himself together. 'But before anything else, I have to bury Candy.'

Scott nodded. 'We can do that together.'

21

Katie continued to wave even after the picture on her computer shrank to nothing.

'Merry Christmas. I love you all,' she whispered again to the family who could no longer see or hear her.

She cancelled Skype and set the computer to playing music. It had been lovely to talk to her family. They didn't seem quite so far away now. She had laughed at the reindeer face on the Christmas jumper her mum had knitted for her big brother. Her dad had loved the Australian stubby holder she had sent him in the post. It was just a cylinder of foam, designed to keep a beer cold. Not a big issue back home right now, where London was looking pretty under a light dusting of snow.

She sighed. She did miss her family, but today had proven one thing to her.

She could manage on her own. Her family would always be there for her whenever she needed them. Their love was steadfast and unconditional. The decision to come to Coorah Creek had not been about her family. It was about a career that was broken and needed fixing. There was no doubt she was feeling better about her chosen path now than she had been the day she walked out of that soulless hospital. There were things she enjoyed about small town nursing. But flying in that air ambulance was not one of them! She shuddered. It didn't matter how long she stayed, she would never get used to that.

But stay she would!

Katie got up and walked to the window to look out across the open spaces that surrounded the hospital. Despite last night's rain, a full day of blazing sun had left the scraggy gum trees looking dusty still. They always looked dusty. Much as she missed England's green and pleasant land, going back now would be a mark of failure. She would stay in Coorah Creek until she had regained her love of nursing. Until she was ready to put her career back on track.

And she would stay because Scott was here. Not in Coorah Creek, but here in Australia. She didn't know where the motor museum was. She guessed it would be in Canberra. That was a long way from Coorah Creek, but not impossible to manage.

She had given up telling herself that it was too soon for her to fall in love with a man who had literally found her on the side of the road. Time didn't matter. Scott had worked his way into her heart and lodged there. The connection between them was stronger than anything she had felt before — and she knew it was not caused by her loneliness or his sadness. Wherever and whenever they had met, they would feel the same.

His stay in Coorah Creek had already been longer than his original plan. He'd stayed because he wanted to make amends with his father. And he'd stayed because of her — she knew that as surely as she knew anything.

Neither of them had said it in so many words — but both of them wanted to give this relationship a chance.

She looked down at her watch. Where was Scott?

It was almost seven o'clock. Scott had been with his father for a couple of hours. She hoped they had finally managed a reconciliation. Feeling restless, she stood up and crossed the room to turn on the overhead fan. The day was still incredibly hot and there wasn't even a breath of wind. Katie glanced out the window to the sinking sun, glinting on the tinsel on her small tree. It was really just a branch pulled from what looked almost like a pine tree in the hospital car park, but it was her way of marking the day. Scott's gift was sitting under the tree. She forced herself to sit down again and pick up a book. Scott would come when he could.

* * *

Scott was sweating freely as he walked towards the hospital. It wasn't a long walk from his old home, but the night was hot. Christmas always involved a lot of sweat. He tried to imagine what it would be like having Christmas in England. Instead of prawns, a steaming roast turkey would be on the menu. Instead of cold beer, maybe hot mulled wine. Instead of blazing sunshine and the chance of a swim in the creek there could be snow. He'd never seen snow. That might be fun.

Just ahead was the sign pointing to the hospital. And a little way off the road, he saw a light glinting. Katie's light, welcoming him. His steps hastened.

When she opened the door, it seemed all the emotions of the past few hours just erupted inside him. He gathered her into his arms and held her as if he would never let her go. He felt as if his body was shaking, and Katie was the only thing keeping him firmly on the ground. The emotional roller coaster of the past few hours had exhausted him. He held her for a long time, before he found the strength to step away.

'Are you all right?' her voice was full of concern as she raised one hand to gently wipe away the hint of a tear on his cheek. 'What happened?'

'Candy, my old dog. The one I left behind. She's been with Dad all these years. She died tonight.'

'Oh Scott, I am so sorry.'

'We . . . we buried her at the back of the garden. It was so strange to be doing something like that together.'

'How's your dad?'

'He's going to be okay. We both are.' He ran his hand over his face. 'I have been wrong about my father for all these years.'

Without a word she took his hand and led him inside. Thankfully he collapsed on her couch — all the while holding her hand like a lifeline.

'I don't know where to start.' He took a deep breath.

She sat quietly while he told her. Tears glinted in her eyes at times, but she never took her blue eyes from his face. He felt her concern and her empathy — dare he say her love — curl around him like a blanket, helping to ease the shock and pain and grief. And slowly, ever so slowly, a strange kind of joy replaced them.

'I guess all these years, subconsciously I thought it was my fault. My mother left me. My father hated me. I thought there was something wrong with me. That I was unlovable.'

'No!' The intensity and certainty of her statement was a balm to his shattered emotions.

'It never occurred to me that my father was struggling to cope with losing the woman he loved. He says that every time he looked at me, he saw her in my eyes. That explains why he was so withdrawn and hard. He was fighting every day to keep himself together.'

'He must have loved her very much.'

'You know, I think maybe he still does. After all these years.' Scott squeezed her hand gently. 'We Collinses are a stubborn lot.'

'That I already knew.'

They both smiled.

'So what happens now?' Katie asked, her voice very soft.

He knew what she was thinking. Would he stay in Coorah Creek or would he leave and take his dream job. She still didn't know quite what 'leaving' meant. It was time he told her.

'I'm going to stay another week or two. Dad wants to do some work around the house and garage. Clean out a lot of old stuff. Smarten it up a bit. I'll help him with that. I think working together will be a good chance to get to know each other again.'

'And then?'

'I'm going to take the job. At the National Motor Museum. It is the fulfilment of a dream for me. Dad understands. He says I have to be true to myself or I'm no good to anyone. He's right. And he says he'll come and visit. It will be fun showing him the cars I'm working on.'

He didn't miss the flash of disappointment in her eyes. But she hid it well. 'Can I come and visit too? Is it in Canberra? It would be exciting to play tourist there too.'

'Of course you can visit, but — ' He hesitated. He should have told her this a long time ago. 'The thing is, Katie, the job is at the National Motor Museum. In England.'

Her face froze for a second. Then she let go of his hand. He felt bereft as she walked to the window to stare out into the darkness. The silence stretched on for a long time before she finally spoke.

'I've been there. It's wonderful. You'll love it.'

'Katie — ' He stood and moved towards her, but not too close. The set of her shoulders told him she needed a little space. 'Come with me. You've always said you would go home to England. Do it now. We can go there together.'

She shook her head. 'I can't leave yet. I have to do this job properly. I need to understand just what I want to do with the rest of my life.'

His heart sank, but he understood. 'You have to be true to yourself too. And when you're ready, I'll still be in England. I'll wait for you.'

She nodded. Her shoulders heaved as she sighed. When she turned back towards him, she had a smile on her face, but he could tell it was forced.

'This makes my present even more appropriate,' she said as she reached for something under her tree. 'I meant this as a joke against my accent. But — '

Her voice trailed away as she handed it to him. He unwrapped the book and read the message inside — carefully crafted out of Australian slang.

To a ridgy-didge Aussie,
You're a bonzer bloke.
With love from your Pommy Sheila.

He wasn't sure whether to laugh or cry.

'I have something for you too.' He reached into his pocket. 'This was my mother's. Dad gave it to me tonight. I'd like you to have it.'

The silver chain glistened in the light as Katie took it. She looked at the small heart nestled in the palm of her hand.

'I'm going to miss you,' she said in a very tiny voice.

'We have two weeks,' Scott said as he gathered her into his arms again. 'We'll figure something out.'

22

Katie couldn't get Scott's words out of her mind. She was supposed to be working, sorting out supplies and making a list for reordering, while at the same time being the only on-call person at the hospital. Adam and Jess had left early that morning on a flight to Birdsville, to pick up a suspected heart attack patient and fly them to Mt Isa. She had felt relieved when Adam told her there was no need for her to come.

She was trying to focus on the job, but her mind was racing. Her feelings toward Scott hadn't changed. If anything, his revelations on Christmas Day had only drawn them closer together. She was so glad he had found what he was searching for, but the thought of being left behind when he went to the UK was devastating. But, at the same time, she couldn't walk away from this job before she'd found what she was looking for.

If you can't be true to yourself —

Her thoughts were interrupted by a screech of tyres as a car entered the car park at high speed. She was on her feet in a second, knowing immediately that there was trouble. Leaving the office she saw Jack North dart through the hospital's front door and hurry down the hallway towards her. She had been in Coorah Creek long enough to know that Jack was the man everyone called on in an emergency. The look on his face left her in no doubt there was something very wrong somewhere.

'Katie, there's been an accident. On the highway. You're needed.' There was no panic in his voice, but a sense of urgency that did not bode well.

'What happened?'

'A car hit a roo. Rolled and hit a tree.'

'How many people?'

'Just the driver.'

'Is he on his way here?'

Jack shook his head. 'He's trapped in the car. Max Delany — the sergeant — called me. Told me to bring you out there.'

For a few seconds, Katie just froze. Go to the scene of the accident? That wasn't how A&E worked. Ambulances brought the injured to the hospital. And there was always a doctor close by to treat them. She couldn't do this on her own. She wasn't qualified. And then there were the legal issues. What would happen if —

She forced herself to stop. She was needed. Someone was hurt and if there was any chance she could help, she had to go.

'Can you tell me anything about his injures?'

'Max said there's a lot of blood. And there's something wrong with his shoulder.'

'Is he conscious?'

'Yes. Max says he's in a lot of pain.'

Katie nodded. She reached for the

224

emergency travel bag that Adam always kept ready to go. She opened it and quickly checked the contents. She had no real idea of what she would need out there, but the essentials were in the bag.

'Let's go,' she said.

It took just over twenty minutes to get there. Twenty minutes of high speed driving. Katie tried not to think about their speed — or what would happen if they too hit a kangaroo in the road. Jack seemed a good driver. She put a lid on her uncertainty and fears and just let herself trust him.

The accident scene was strangely still. The police car was parked on the side of the road, its lights flashing. There were two other vehicles there — passers-by who had stopped to help. It seemed strange that there was no ambulance. No fire engines. No tow trucks. Just ordinary people ready to help if they were needed.

Katie grabbed the bag from the back of the car and hurried towards a white station wagon that lay against a big gum tree a few yards off the road. The car would have rolled onto its roof, had the tree not stopped it. Instead it rested at a crazy angle — not quite upside down, but not on its side either. She knew in an instant that getting the driver out was going to be difficult and possibly dangerous. As she approached, she noticed a bloody shape lying in the long brown grass not too far away. The kangaroo. She barely had time to hope the poor creature hadn't suffered, when the police sergeant hurried to her.

'The driver's still in the car,' Delany said.

'Is he conscious?' she asked.

'Yes. He's in a lot of pain. And he's bleeding from multiple cuts.'

Katie started to move, but Max grabbed her arm.

'Be careful. The car is resting against the tree. It's not safe. We need to get him out of there before you can treat him.'

'I understand. But I need to see him before you try to move him.'

226

Max hesitated and then nodded.

Swiftly but carefully, Katie approached the car. All she could see was the underside of the vehicle. One wheel was missing and parts of the exhaust were hanging off.

A man screamed in agony.

In a trice, Katie was crouched beside the vehicle, broken glass crunching beneath her feet as she spoke to the injured driver who was still strapped in his seat, his body trapped and twisted inside the mangled metal.

'It's going to be all right. My name is Katie and I'm here to help.'

A bloodstained face slowly turned towards her, and Katie was shocked to see how very young the man was.

'What's your name?'

'Tom,' the voice was harsh with agony, but he seemed to have his wits about him.

'Hi Tom.' Katie quickly scanned the young man's body. There was a lot of blood, but the wounds seemed mostly superficial. It was his shoulder that worried her. 'Can you move your hands?'

He grunted with effort. Or with pain.

'The . . . one hand yes. The other one
. . . left arm . . . ' His voice trailed off.

'Don't worry, Tom. We'll have you
out of there in a minute.'

Katie stood and backed away from
the injured man. Max and Jack were
waiting. They were holding what looked
like welding gear.

'We can cut him out now, if it's safe
to move him,' Max said.

'I'll put a neck brace on him before
you start. I think his back is okay, but
you've got to be gentle.'

'Are you going to give him something?'

The young man groaned again, and
Katie's heart sank. 'He needs pain medi-
cation, but I'm not qualified . . . not
allowed to give him morphine . . . or
anything that will do much good.'

'But we're going to have to lift him
out . . . ' Max said.

'I know,' she almost yelled. 'But I
can't. Only a doctor can prescribe — '

She was interrupted by a sound from behind her. The radio on the police car crackled and she heard indistinct voices.

'You have radio contact?' she asked Max.

'Yes. With regional base.'

'Could they get in touch with a Doctor. Maybe call Adam in the plane. He can authorise . . . ' Max turned before she finished speaking. While he returned to his car, Katie pulled a neck brace from the emergency bag. She tried to avoid causing Tom any more pain as she fitted it, telling him all the while that it would help protect him and that the men would have him out very soon. Her heart shrank every time he cried out in pain.

Just as she finished, Max called her back to the police car and placed his radio in her hand.

'It's Adam. He's on the plane on his way back.'

Relief surged through her. 'How far out are you?' she said into the handset.

'Forty minutes until we land. Then we'd have to get to you.' Adam's voice was distorted by the radio. 'How is he?'

'Not good. He's in a lot of pain and looks like a dislocated shoulder. I've got a neck brace on him, but he's going to need pain meds if they are going to drag him out of there.'

'You're right. In the bag. Everything you need is there.'

Max quickly fetched the bag. Following Adam's instructions, she found the small vials of morphine. And the syringe. She checked the dose with him twice while Max listened.

'All right. Do it. Then get him out of the car. You can call me back then if you need to. Good Luck.'

She didn't allow herself to hesitate. She administered the morphine and with a final reassuring word to the injured youth, she stepped back and let Jack and Max do what they had to. Sparks flew as they cut away the car door and the front pillar. The car seemed even more fragile now, and more dangerous.

'Watch his shoulder' she said. The two men followed her instructions carefully and pulled her patient from the car. The morphine had taken affect, but still he screamed.

Katie was beside him in an instant. His eyes were unfocused with a combination of drugs and the pain. She carefully touched the hand that hung uselessly from his dislocated shoulder. It was cold. That wasn't good.

She drew Jack and Max aside.

'I'm worried about that shoulder. It's pinching the main blood vessel. If we don't fix it, he could lose the hand.'

'What do you need us to do?' Jack asked.

'Brace him. I have to put that shoulder back in. I need you to hold him down and still. I have to apply a lot of pressure to do it.'

Both men nodded and dropped to their knees beside Tom. Katie didn't stop to think. She'd been taught about this. Seen it done a dozen times before, but never done it herself. This young man needed her to get it right the first time.

She made sure Jack and Max had a firm hold on her patient, then she lifted his arm. Despite the drugs, he whimpered in pain as she slowly began to pull and twist the arm. It seemed an eternity. Just as she began to think she was doing something wrong, the shoulder slipped back into place.

After that, things moved quickly.

Katie strapped Tom's arm and shoulder to prevent too much movement as they loaded him into the police Land Rover to take him back to Coorah Creek. She rode with him, dressing his cuts and talking to him as they went. In the front of the car, Max was attempting to contact Adam.

Just as they approached the road leading to the airstrip outside town, Adam's car emerged. It turned towards them and accelerated for a few seconds before the driver recognised the police car. As they flashed past, Katie saw Adam's face. He flung the car into a high-speed U-turn and followed them back to the hospital.

'Let's get him inside,' he ordered the moment the cars pulled up in front of the building. 'I'll get him stabilised while Jess refuels the plane, and then we'll get him to the Isa for a CAT scan.'

As Jack half carried their patient up the steps to the hospital, Adam paused next to Katie for just a second.

'Well done,' he said.

23

'I was scared, you know. Really scared!'

'Climbing inside that damaged car should have scared you. You could have been hurt.'

'No. Not scared for me. Scared for him. That I wouldn't be able to help him. But I did.'

The smile on Katie's face grew even bigger; if that was possible. She was almost bursting with pleasure as she sat opposite Scott in the pub, waiting for their dinner to be served. This was what had been missing from her life. This feeling of achievement. That she had helped someone using her own skill and wits.

'Oh Scott,' she grabbed his hand. 'This is why I became a nurse. I was able to help someone. Adam said I saved his arm. Me!'

Scott's face told her everything she

needed to know. He was both impressed and proud. Come to think of it, she felt exactly the same way.

'Here you go,' Ed appeared, three glasses clutched in his hand. He placed the drinks on the table and sat down with them.

'Here's to you,' Scott raised his glass. 'Well done.'

'Yes, well done indeed.' Ed smiled and for a moment Katie put aside her excitement at her own achievement. Here was another reason to celebrate. Scott and his father were beginning to act like they were not just a family, but friends too. She was so happy for him. For all of them. Right now, life was good. Her joy clouded for a moment as she thought of the parting that was ahead of them, in just a few days when Scott headed for his new job. But she shook it off. Nothing was going to spoil this moment for her.

'Hey, Katie!' Max appeared, still wearing his police uniform. 'I've just heard from Adam. The patient is doing fine. He and Jess will be flying back tomorrow after they check in one last time at the hospital. They should be back shortly after lunch. They asked you to hold the fort at the hospital for them.'

'That's good news. As for holding the fort, I'll do my best. But please,' Katie grinned, 'no more adventures like today.'

'And if there were, I'm sure you'd do fine,' Trish appeared carrying plates loaded down with food. She placed them on the table, grinning at the three of them as if she were in some way responsible for the aura of happiness that surrounded them. 'If you keep this up girl, we'll be calling you Doctor Katie.'

They all laughed, but as Trish moved away, Scott suddenly fell silent.

'What's wrong?' Katie asked.

He didn't answer. His mouth curved into a knowing smile and he raised his eyebrows.

'What!'

Still he didn't answer. Realisation dawned suddenly.

'No,' she said. 'It's a nice idea, but it will never happen.'

'Why not?' Scott asked.

'Just because.'

'Do you want to let me in on this conversation?' Ed asked.

'Katie's going to become a doctor,' Scott said.

Katie shook her head. 'Don't be silly. I'm a nurse, not a doctor.'

Scott leaned forward, his eyes shining with excitement. 'But you could be a doctor. You told me that's what you wanted to be. You said nursing wasn't as fulfilling as you wanted. That's because you should be a doctor. You were born for it!'

'It's a nice thought, Scott,' Katie said. 'And a compliment. Thank you. But it's not going to happen. So come on. Eat that burger before it gets cold.'

She followed her own advice, and began eating. During the rest of the evening, Scott's words hovered in the back of her mind. Quite a few townsfolk dropped by to hear the story of the rescue, which by now had grown to epic proportions. Any minute, Katie was expecting someone to ask her about single-handedly pulling the victim from a burning wreck. Obviously the Trish Warren gossip grapevine was flourishing.

It was quite late when they finally made their escape. The three of them walked across the road to Ed's house. After just a couple of days, it was already showing the results of Ed and Scott's work. The garden had been cut back and there was fresh paint appearing on the outside of the house.

'I'll say goodnight,' Ed said. Almost shyly he leaned forward to kiss Katie's cheek softly. 'You did a good thing today Katie. We are all very proud of you.'

'Thanks,' she said, deeply moved.

'Goodnight son. And take good care of this girl. She's special.' Ed placed a hand on his son's shoulder for a few seconds and then turned away.

'I think he's a nice man,' Katie said

as she took Scott's hand and turned their steps towards the hospital. 'He just hasn't had much of a chance to show it.'

'I know.'

They walked in silence for a while. Katie looked up at the stars shining so brilliantly above her. She never saw stars like that in London.

'Do you really think I could do it?' she said.

Scott squeezed her hand. 'Of course you could.'

'But . . . a doctor?'

'Why not?'

'For a start, there's the question of money,' Katie said. 'It'll be expensive to go back to college.'

'Are there grants or scholarships or something you can apply for?' Scott asked.

'I guess so. But — '

'No buts,' he said firmly. 'We'll make it work. I can help you.'

'I'm just — '

Scott stopped and turned her to face

him. His handsome face looked very intense in the bright starlight. 'You are not 'just' anything Katie Brooks. You are a smart and determined woman. You can be or do whatever you want.'

'I don't know.'

'But I do.' Then he kissed her.

It was several minutes before they resumed their walk. Katie's mind was racing.

'You know, a couple of the nurses I trained with went on to study medicine,' she said. 'It's not totally impossible.'

'There you go.'

'Of course,' she felt a smile spreading across her face as the doubt began to fade, 'I would have to go back to the UK to do this.'

'I thought that might be the case. You'll have to resign from this job.'

'I'm sure Adam can find someone else. And Jess will be pleased that I'm not being ill in her aeroplane any more.'

'She's not the only one who'll be pleased to see you heading back to England.'

'But Scott, it won't be easy to BE us. I'll be in London. You'll be at the Museum. And I'll be working ridiculous hours. Studying. I won't have time . . . '

'It doesn't matter,' Scott said. 'Don't look for the barriers. That's what I have done for the past few years with Dad, and it was wrong. Whatever you need to do, you do it. I'll be there when I can and I will give you space when you need it. I'll support you every step of the way and no-one will be happier than me to see you in a black robe on your graduation day.'

They had reached the steps to the hospital. An outside light was on and Katie could see the sincerity in Scott's face as he spoke.

'You're a nice man too,' she said and kissed him.

24

Katie's old car had polished up pretty well. Ed flicked a cleaning rag at a bit of imaginary dust, proud of his handiwork. The grey Prius was parked nearby. Scott squeezed the last box into the boot and shut the lid. He leaned over to rub at the thin scratch on his rear bumper, smiling as he remembered the day that happened.

'Thanks for offering to sell Katie's car,' he said as he joined Ed. 'It would have been a pain to have to take two cars back east.'

'No problems. I've got a buyer in mind. And you can trust me to get the best price I can.'

'I know. She's going to need the money. Medical school will be expensive.'

'On that note,' Ed hesitated. His son was a proud man and he didn't want to offend him. 'I've been living here, alone for a long time. I don't make a lot of money, but I don't spend much either. I have some savings. If you or Katie need money . . . '

Scott shook his head. 'Thanks for the offer Dad. But no. We can do this. Why don't you spend that money on coming over to England for a visit. I'd love to show you the cars.'

'I'll be there,' Ed said. 'But if you change your mind, don't hesitate to ask.'

Scott nodded.

'And I've come to a decision about my own life,' Ed continued. 'I've been waiting all these years for something that is never going to happen and it's time to stop.'

'What are you going to do?'

'I'm going to hire a lawyer. Maybe he can find your mother. Maybe not. But either way it's time I started living my life again. I'm not that old. Maybe there's someone else out there for me after all.'

On the other side of the main road, Katie appeared in the doorway of the town store. She was carrying a couple of plastic bags; supplies for their journey. She darted across to the front of the pub, where Trish Warren was waiting. The two women hugged.

A slow smile across Scott's face as he watched them

'You take good care of that girl,' Ed said. 'She is something special.'

'I know. I think I finally understand what you said about falling in love with Mum right from the moment you met. It must run in the family.'

'Scott. Catch.'

He responded by instinct and neatly caught the bottle of water Katie had tossed at him as she approached. Laughing, she held up a six pack of the clear liquid she had just purchased at the store.

'Well — you've gained something from this whole experience,' Scott joked.

'Yes, I have,' Katie paused long enough

to plant a gentle kiss on his cheek before opening the door to stash the water on the back seat of the Prius.

'All set?' Ed asked.

'Yes.' Katie came around the car and enveloped Ed in a bear hug. 'Thanks for everything.'

'No. I have a lot to thank you for.' Ed spoke softly as he returned her hug. 'I'll miss you both.' He said something else too, but Scott couldn't hear him.

Katie rubbed a damp eye and nodded as she stepped back.

'Dad.' There was a lump in Scott's throat. He had never wanted to return to Coorah Creek — but now he was finding it hard to leave.

Ed stepped forward to hug his son.

'I love you Dad,' Scott whispered.

'I love you too, Son.' The two men hugged for a few seconds more, and then stepped away from each other.

'All right you two, time you were on your way.' Ed ran a hand roughly over his face.

'You know, just now Trish told me

she knew of some puppies that were available,' Katie said, trying to hide a sniff. 'You should think about getting a new dog.'

'No. I'm not really a dog person. That was all Scott's fault.' Ed smiled slowly. 'I was thinking I might get a cat. Just don't let Trish know. Okay?'

They both nodded and with a last long look around, Scott slid behind the wheel of his car. A few moments later, he turned the key and slowly, drew away from the garage.

He kept their speed down as they moved through the town. Scott looked at the place he'd grown up through new eyes.

'You're going to miss this place, you know,' Katie said. 'And your Dad.'

'I know. Dad says he might come and visit in the English summer. After we've had time to settle down.'

'Great. He whispered something to you . . . what?'

Scott cast a sideways glance at the beautiful woman beside him. 'He told me to look after you.'

Katie smiled. 'He told me the same thing.'

The town was starting to recede in the background. 'It was good of Adam to let you go like this,' Scott said. 'I was expecting you'd have to wait longer.'

'I think Jess convinced him it was for the best. They've already advertised for someone new.'

A road sign flashed past. Looking in his rear view mirror, Scott saw it was the town sign. Even in mirror image, he could read the words. Coming back to the Coorah Creek had changed his life for the better. He was setting out on a new adventure, but he would be back. Maybe one day Katie and he would bring their kids here. He'd like to show them the outback.

They drove for a little while each of them lost in their own thoughts. Then Scott let his speed drop and eased towards the side of the road.

'What's wrong?' Katie asked.

'Nothing.' The car stopped. Scott got

out and walked round to open Katie's door. Looking confused she got out.

'Do you remember this spot?' he asked.

She looked around. 'Was this where I broke down?'

'More or less.'

'Wow. She reached out to take his hand. 'It wasn't all that long ago.'

'Officially it was last year.'

'True, but a lot has changed in a very short time. I can hardly believe I'm going home.'

'That we are going home.'

'It's a little scary,' Katie said in a small voice. 'This medical school thing. I'm still a little afraid of that.'

'Don't be. Ambition is a good thing. Reach for the stars. I am.'

'What stars are you reaching for?'

He took her hand and kissed it. 'I think you know. I know I found something special on the side of this road that day. We haven't known each other very long, but I think this is just a beginning for us. We can take this as fast or as slow as you like . . . but I think I already know where our road is leading.'

Katie's heart skipped a beat. 'Be careful what you wish for,' she said with a smile. 'You might get it.'

Laughing, they got back into the car, and before he started the engine, Scott kissed her.

'I love you,' he said.

He started the engine and the car leaped forward. It quickly gathered speed and vanished into the silver heat haze shimmering across the thin strip of grey road.

We do hope that you have enjoyed reading this large print book.

Did you know that all of our titles are available for purchase?

We publish a wide range of high quality large print books including:
Romances, Mysteries, Classics
General Fiction
Non Fiction and Westerns

Special interest titles available in large print are:
The Little Oxford Dictionary
Music Book, Song Book
Hymn Book, Service Book

Also available from us courtesy of Oxford University Press:
Young Readers' Dictionary
(large print edition)
Young Readers' Thesaurus
(large print edition)

For further information or a free brochure, please contact us at:
Ulverscroft Large Print Books Ltd.,
The Green, Bradgate Road, Anstey,
Leicester, LE7 7FU, England.
Tel: (00 44) **0116 236 4325**
Fax: (00 44) **0116 234 0205**

Other titles in the
Linford Romance Library:

THE BRIDESMAID'S ROYAL BODYGUARD

Liz Fielding

After being sacked from her job with a gossip magazine, Ally Parker is given a fresh start when her childhood friend Hope asks her to work PR for her marriage to Prince Jonas of San Michele. When Count Fredrik Jensson, head of security for the royal family, arrives, he makes it clear that Ally's past employment makes her unfit for her role. The fact that there's a sizzle between them from the moment they meet only makes everything worse . . .

PAWS FOR LOVE

Sarah Purdue

Sam rescues animals and trains assistance dogs — but has less understanding of people! Meanwhile, Henry is desperate to help his young son Toby, who hasn't spoken since his mother died. Toby's therapist has suggested that an assistance dog might help the boy. Unfortunately, Henry Wakefield is terrified of dogs! But when Sam brings Juno into their lives, Toby begins to blossom and Henry starts to relax. Will Juno prove to be a large and hairy Cupid for Sam and Henry?

ALWAYS THE BRIDESMAID

Jo Bartlett

Finally moving home after five years in Australia waiting in vain for faithless Josh, Olivia is welcomed back into the heart of her best friend's family on the Kent coast. Cakes, donkeys, weddings and a fulfilling summer job — all is wonderful, except for her unsettling attraction to Seth, who is moving to the United States after the summer. Is it worth taking a chance on love, or would it just lead to more heartbreak?

CORA'S CHRISTMAS KISS

Alison May

Cora and Liam have both experienced horrible years that have led them to the same unlikely place — spending December working in the grotto at Golding's department store. Under the cover of a Father Christmas fat suit and an extremely unflattering reindeer costume, they find comfort in sharing their tales of woe during their bleak staffroom lunch breaks. But is their new-found friendship just for Christmas? Or have they created something deeper, something that could carry them through to a hopeful new year?